Praise for *Chrissy's Cozy Mystery Series*

First responders are almost never really off the clock. Even on weekends or vacations, there is invariably a car at the side of the road, a person lost or injured, a sudden bank robbery—happened more than once to me. Ray and Autumn face the recent crises together when a missing person situation becomes a complex series of mysteries and whodunnits. A bit of honeymoon sweet stuff, and a whole lot of craziness—and of course Chrissy and Ace the majestic and fabulous pet companions.

—Molly G. Hamblin

The latest installment of the Chrissy the Shih Tzu cozy mysteries, finds Lieutenant Ray Reed and his wife of five months, Autumn Clarke Reed finally taking time to go on their honeymoon. They head to the Poconos with their two dogs, Chrissy and Ace, anticipating two weeks of rest, relaxation, good food, and intimacy. Instead, on their first day in a quaint, cozy cabin on a lake, a dead body floats in the water a few yards away from their dock. I really enjoyed meeting new characters and following the plot twists. Every time a new character was introduced, I thought, "Oh, he/she is the killer!" only to find out I was wrong. I also suspected a few innocent characters and was truly surprised when the true murderer was revealed. I highly recommend this cute, cozy mystery.

—Terri Chalmers, New Jersey

I absolutely love *Doggone Honeymoon*, the fifth installment in Diane Wing's cozy mystery series. Grab a cup of tea, soft blanket and set aside a Sunday afternoon to enjoy the light-suspenseful, jaw-dropping, intriguing plot twist with lovable, huggable characters of Autumn and Chrissy, Ray and Ace. You don't have to be a dog lover to appreciate these mysterious adventures of whodunnit!

—Annette Sadelson, Maryland

I am always amazed by Diane's plot twisting murder mysteries. Her storyline makes me suspect every single character at least once until I am still genuinely surprised to find out who dunnit in the end!

—Antoinette B. Leonardtown, MD

A killer is loose at Moonlight Lake. Diane Wing takes her *Chrissy's Mysteries* series to new heights in *Doggone Honeymoon*, a fresh and highly entertaining read with twists and turns that will surprise and confound even the most experienced reader's 'Inner Sleuth.' This book will keep you spellbound until the final page is turned. Prepare to limit unnecessary interruptions while enjoying this exciting new cozy mystery.

Autumn and her new husband, Ray Reed, set off for a peaceful long-awaited honeymoon at Moonlight Lake with their canine companions, Chrissy the Shih Tzu and Ace, the retired German Shepherd police dog. Their tranquil holiday quickly becomes a grim working vacation when Ace finds the body of a local woman floating in the lake near their rented cabin. Ray and Autumn join forces with the Stroudsburg Police to assist the investigation, and quickly uncover odd and complicated relationships between the colorful local residents who all harbor their own secrets and possible motives.

Don't miss this book! Join Autumn, Ray, Chrissy, and Ace as they uncover the many secrets hidden in plain sight, find the murderer, and enjoy their *Doggone Honeymoon*!

—Maxine Ashcraft, California

This series has a calming effect on me. The author does a wonderful job of writing a page turning mystery that you can get lost in for hours. Even though it is a work of fiction, when you put the book down you feel renewed and refreshed. There is a lot of character development in this series and I enjoy seeing how the characters have developed throughout the three books. I am looking forward to seeing where the author takes the series next!

—Marie McNary, *A Cozy Experience*

I loved getting to know the characters better, their interactions and the motives that drive them. The dogs however need a special mention from the stoic guardian Ace to the adorable, clue sniffing Chrissy and their utter commitment to the humans that they have taken under their paw.

—*Krystyna's Reviews*

!

DOGGONE HONEYMOON

A Chrissy the
Shih Tzu Cozy Mystery

DIANE WING

Modern History Press

Ann Arbor, MI

ISBN 978-1-61599-848-7 paperback
ISBN 978-1-61599-849-4 hardcover
ISBN 978-1-61599-850-0 eBook

Published by
Modern History Press   www.ModernHistoryPress.com
5145 Pontiac Trail   info@ModernHistoryPress.com
Ann Arbor, MI   tollfree 888-761-6268

Distributed by Ingram (USA/CAN/AU), Bertram's Books (UK/EU)

To my incredible husband and two snuggly fur babies.
I'm very fortunate to be surrounded by so much love.

Books by Diane Wing....

Cozy Mysteries with Chrissy the Shih Tzu

Attorney-at-Paw

The Dog-Eared Diary

Trick-or-Doggy Treat

A Winter's Tail

Doggone Honeymoon

Dark Fantasy

Coven: The Scrolls of the Four Winds

Thorne Manor and other bizarre tales

Trips to the Edge: Tales of the Unexpected

Forest of the Dead: Stories of Transformation

Non-fiction

The True Nature of Tarot: Your Path to Personal Empowerment, 10th Anniversary Ed.

The True Nature of Energy: Transforming Anxiety into Tranquility

The Happiness Perspective: Seeing Your Life Differently

Contents

Dramatis Personae

Locals on the Scene

Amy Armstrong—Loretta Armstrong's mother.

Barry Armstrong—Amy Armstrong's husband.

Loretta Armstrong—Victim, Madison's sister, Amy Armstrong's daughter.

Madison Armstrong—Loretta Armstrong's sister.

Cathy Bailey—Loretta Armstrong's roommate.

Monica Bailey—Cathy Bailey's mother.

Danny Cole—Bartender at the Log Cabin Bar and friend of Loretta Armstrong.

Lily Harding—Loretta Armstrong's co-worker at the Tall Tree Restaurant.

Miguel Lopez—Owns canoe and kayak rental business on Moonlight Lake.

Bobby Ringbottom—Loretta Armstrong's boyfriend.

Harley Waters—Loretta Armstrong's boss at Harley's General Store.

Local Law Enforcement

Ross Adams—Detective with Knollwood police.

Officer Christine Campos—Law enforcement in Stroudsburg.

John Conroy—Detective with Stroudsburg Police.

Officer Alison Williams—Law enforcement in Stroudsburg.

Autumn Clarke Reed's Family and Friends

Kirby Galloway—Local dog groomer.

Autumn Clarke Reed—Chrissy's pet parent and wife of Ray Reed.

Ray Reed—Lieutenant with Knollwood police, husband of Autumn Reed, and pet parent of Ace.

Maureen Roberts—Autumn's Realtor.

Ace—Ray's retired police dog (German Shepherd Dog).

Chrissy—Autumn's dog and pet detective (Shih Tzu).

Missing Persons Report—Knollwood, PA

Loretta Armstrong, 28, was reported missing by her mother, Amy Armstrong, after she didn't come home from a night out with friends. She was last seen at the River Café in New Hope, PA on May 6, 2024, wearing a red plaid flannel shirt and jeans. Her mother expected her home afterward. Loretta came down from her home in East Stroudsburg, PA to visit her parents for the weekend. She was driving a silver 2019 Toyota Corolla. Loretta is Caucasian, with long black hair and blue eyes. She's 5' 6" with a medium build. Please call the Knollwood Police Department at 215-555-9147 with any information.

≈ 1 ≈

Waiting five months to go on their honeymoon was an exercise in patience. In the meantime, Autumn Reed busied herself with building her bed-and-breakfast business and researching rental properties close to home in the Pocono Mountains. Her husband, Lieutenant Ray Reed, worked at the Knollwood police department conducting criminal investigations and overseeing detectives and officers. He told Autumn to choose the place. He didn't care where, as long as they were together. Ray had punctuated this statement with a deep kiss that sent chills down Autumn's spine. She smiled, remembering the moment, feeling her love for Ray bubble up.

Autumn knew the primary criteria was a peaceful getaway with their dogs, Chrissy, a Shih Tzu, and Ace, a German Shepherd Dog, who was Ray's retired law enforcement partner. The couple took their dogs with them ninety-eight percent of the time. There were few occasions that required Chrissy and Ace to stay home, such as a formal dinner event, which Ray was sometimes required to attend for official reasons. As a lieutenant of the Knollwood police department, the mayor and other political officials in his township, and sometimes in neighboring jurisdictions, expected him to schmooze and to bring his wealthy wife. No dogs allowed.

With their busy lives, and the fact that they were newlyweds, Autumn and Ray looked forward to time alone to snuggle, talk about their dreams and hopes for the future, and to have as many intimate romantic encounters as they could over their two-week vacation. And, of course, play with the pups.

Not having much luck online, she called Amy Armstrong, a longtime friend of Autumn's mother, Stella Clarke, who checked on Autumn from time to time after Stella died in a car accident. Amy had a vacation house in Stroudsburg, so she called her for guidance on a rental property. Luck was with them. A rental had just come up, and Amy knew the owners. It was a great pet-friendly cottage with ample space, floor to ceiling windows, and a private dock right on Moonlight Lake in East Stroudsburg, a neighboring town to where Amy's house was. After seeing photos, Autumn and Ray booked the place for May, thinking the spring weather would be nice around that time and it was before the tourist season officially started.

Autumn was packing for the trip when the phone rang. Caller ID showed it was Amy Armstrong.

"Hey, Amy," Autumn answered, and then listened.

"She's missing?" Autumn asked, feeling the worry of Loretta Armstrong's mother at the other end of the phone line.

"I saw her last night before she went to meet friends at the River Cafe for dinner," said Amy. Now she was the one who needed support.

"Have you notified the Knollwood police?"

"Not yet. It hasn't been twenty-four hours. I was hoping Ray could ask around for me."

"The waiting period is a myth. Call the police right away and give them all the information you have, including the names of the friends she was meeting last night."

"Okay."

"I'll let Ray know you'll be calling. Keep me posted."

"I will, dear. Thank you."

They disconnected the call, and Autumn dialed Ray to give him the news.

Chrissy, Autumn's gray and white Shih Tzu, trotted into the kitchen and looked up at her mommy. A purple satin bow held the topknot in place, keeping the hair out of her eyes. That face made Autumn's heart melt every time. She lifted her up and snuggled her close.

"We need to help Amy find Loretta," she whispered in Chrissy's ear and kissed the side of her face. "Let's take a ride."

It was in the upper sixties and clear, nice weather for early May in Eastern Pennsylvania. Chrissy stepped into her harness and waited for Autumn to clip the leash to the metal loop. Autumn lifted her fur baby into the doggy seat secured to the backseat of the SUV. With her seatbelt fastened, she looked back at Chrissy to make sure she was comfortable, and headed to the River Café to see what she could find out.

She drove cautiously in case something triggered her posttraumatic stress reaction from the car accident that killed her parents. Therapy and Chrissy's diligence in keeping her grounded cleared much of the anxiety, but her careful nature compelled her to be a safe driver.

The tree-lined road heading toward the restaurant was full of deer and other animals, so Autumn stayed vigilant in case any of them darted across the street. Even in daylight, their behavior was unpredictable, and, sadly, plenty of them met with a speeding vehicle. They'd be especially hard to see in the dark until the last minute. Maybe Loretta swerved to avoid a deer and hit a tree. God forbid. She looked side-to-side in case Loretta was walking home. Maybe she had car trouble or, worst case, an accident. But wouldn't she call her mother for a ride if that were the case? Unless her battery was dead. Or she was unconscious.

Autumn turned her mind toward more optimistic scenarios and kept on the lookout for movement. In the rearview mirror, Chrissy looked enthralled by the scenery moving past the window. If she saw Loretta, Autumn was certain she'd bark.

They arrived at the River Café and spoke to the hostess, who admired and petted Chrissy as Autumn held her. She remembered a group of people from last night, because they were loud, laughing and drinking, until one of them, a female fitting Loretta's description, strode past the hostess station, angrily talking to someone on the phone. She told whoever was on the other end that she'd be home in a couple of days, then stomped back to the table. The hostess saw the woman's friends trying to comfort her, rubbing her back and leaning in to hear what happened. They left about ten o'clock.

Autumn and Chrissy got back in the car and called Ray to give him the update.

"I'm going to drive farther north to see if I can spot her car."

"Be careful, please. We don't know what happened or if there may be someone else involved."

"Okay," Autumn assured him.

"There are a couple detectives on the case, so let them do their jobs. I don't want anything to happen to you and Chrissy. Besides, don't you want to pack for our honeymoon? Five months is long enough to wait."

"Agreed. It's long overdue. I can't wait to be alone with you. We don't leave until tomorrow, so I have the afternoon and evening to finish packing."

Autumn traveled about four miles before she spotted Loretta's silver Toyota Corolla on the side of the road. She parked and looked inside, not touching anything. No one was in the car. She didn't test the door to see if it was locked, in case the police could get fingerprints and other evidence from the vehicle.

After giving Ray an update, she left a message for Amy Armstrong while she waited for a police officer to arrive. To her surprise, Ray and Ace arrived at the same time as the patrol car and pulled up behind him. Autumn walked Chrissy over to greet them. Her tail wagged furiously when she saw them.

"Nice to see you in the middle of the day," said Autumn. She admired the way his suit fell across his muscular, lean body and took advantage when the patrol officer turned away, planting a solid kiss on his lips. Even though they were married, she showed respect for his position as lieutenant. "I left a message on Amy's phone letting her know we found Loretta's car. She may be out looking for her."

"I can't imagine what she's going through," said Ray, petting Chrissy's fluffy head, avoiding the purple satin bow.

Ace came over to sniff Chrissy, who wagged her tail. Autumn scratched Ace behind his ears.

"I'm going home to pack. I hope you find Loretta."

"Me, too. We've already notified law enforcement north and south of here. I'll call when we're on our way home."

"It's close to dinnertime. How about I take Ace home with me and feed them?" she said to Ray, and then to Ace in a sweet voice, "Want to head home with me and get some dinner?"

Ace pounded his tail on the ground and trotted over to Autumn's car. Ray smiled.

"He's so smart, it's scary sometimes."

"That's my boy," said Ray in his proud papa voice.

Autumn's phone rang on the way home. It was Amy.

"Thanks for finding Loretta's car, Autumn. No sign of her, though, right?"

"Unfortunately, no. Ray is working with multiple jurisdictions to keep an eye out for her."

"Maybe she went back to her apartment in East Stroudsburg. I just wish she'd call me. Barry and I are heading to our place up there, just in case."

Autumn had met Amy's husband, Barry, only once and tried to remember what he looked like. She'd likely meet him when they were in the mountains.

"Ray and I are leaving to go up there tomorrow, so we'll be nearby if you need anything."

"You've both waited so long for this. I don't want to intrude."

"Finding Loretta is what's important right now."

Autumn thought about Amy's missing daughter. She had a bad feeling about this, but until they found her body, there was hope she was alive.

Watching the early morning mist on the lake behind the cozy mountain cabin Autumn and Ray rented was exactly what she needed. A few cottages dotted the shoreline across the lake. Tucked into the maple, oak, and pine trees, they looked like a painting. The morning air had a touch of crispness, perfect for shorts and a cozy sweater. She took a sip of steaming black tea and sighed.

Their wedding had been perfect. Marrying the man of her dreams and being accepted into his loving family was everything she ever wanted. She felt her parents were there in spirit. They would have loved Ray. And now their delayed honeymoon, with two darling fur babies, in a picture-perfect setting was the whipped cream and a cherry on top of a hot fudge sundae. How did she get so lucky?

Chrissy stared at the water from the comfort of a fluffy pink dog bed set on a waterproof tarp they brought down to the dock. She looked, unfazed, at the squirrel flipping his tail in a red maple tree.

A few feet from Chrissy, Ace sat at attention; his gaze unwavering from the lake. In this unfamiliar environment, a day hadn't been long enough for him to relax. Autumn wasn't sure that Ace ever let his guard down. Between his training and protective instincts, she always felt safe with him around. Ace stayed alert to potential threats until he was certain his family was safe. It was the nature of German Shepherd Dogs to be vigilant and protective. Autumn was glad he kept vigilant, so she didn't have to. Ace sniffed the air. A canoe with a single passenger floated by, too far to pose a threat, yet Ace's intimidating stare followed the boat, warning it not to come closer, until it was no longer a danger to his family.

The sound of the sliding door opening and closing turned Autumn's attention to Ray, bringing out a tray of the thickest French toast she'd ever seen.

"That looks scrumptious!" Autumn said, as she made room for the tray on the table.

Ray set it down humming the tune *Truly Scrumptious* from *Chitty Chitty Bang Bang*, wrapped Autumn in his arms, tilted her backwards, and kissed Autumn so she felt it down to her toes. He righted her, smiled and winked, and sat down. He scanned the lake and took a deep breath. Spring was a peaceful time in the mountain community of East Stroudsburg. Driving up to the Poconos was

Ray's idea and, despite their last misadventure in the mountains of Pennsylvania, Autumn agreed.

"I can't think of a better place for our honeymoon. Quiet," said Ray.

Water lapped the dock and the tiny pebbled beach.

"Two weeks of bliss. I'm glad we waited to go on our honeymoon. If we really like it up here, we can always buy a cabin. It's easier vacationing like this than flying someplace with the pups."

Ray nodded, chewing a piece of French toast. "And we could leave our clothes, dog beds, and other stuff without having to pack every time we want to get away."

They ate breakfast in comfortable silence. The lake's beauty, the gentle sounds of nature, the scent of leafing trees and decaying pine needles, and the lovely surrounding hills filled their senses. Chrissy hopped out of her doggy bed and trotted over to Autumn. She stared until Autumn lifted the sweet pup onto her lap.

Ace let out a low growl, his warning tentative as he assessed the situation. He stood, his head stretching toward the lake. Ray stood to see what Ace was reacting to.

"What is it, boy? A fish?"

Ace let out a loud bark of alarm, making Chrissy and Autumn jump. Chrissy's pink satin bow went wonky on her head, so Autumn unclipped it and tossed it on the table. Ray jogged down to the dock where Ace stood to get a better look. Something floated about fifteen yards away. Squinting, Ray couldn't make out what it was. Ace was on full alert, his barking more urgent.

"Okay, okay."

Ray stepped into the canoe so he could get closer. Ace jumped in behind him.

Autumn squinted and held Chrissy close. She watched as Ray paddled away, Ace no longer barking but still on high alert.

Ray pulled up alongside the mass and poked it with the paddle. Ace was practically on top of Ray, looking over his shoulder. A cloudy blue eye glinted from beneath long, dark hair littered with pine needles and twigs. Looking back at the lovely little cabin, his beautiful wife, and sweet furry pup, he knew their serene honeymoon had just turned into an investigation. He looked up at Autumn and shook his head as he reached for his cell phone to dial 911 and then called the detective he left in charge in Knollwood.

Local News, East Stroudsburg, PA—Body found in Moonlight Lake

The body of Loretta Armstrong was found this morning, May 8, 2024, floating in Moonlight Lake. Her mother reported her missing a week ago in Knollwood, PA. If you have information regarding this case, please contact the East Stroudsburg Police.

If anyone told Autumn that their honeymoon would include a dead body, she would have waved them away as being silly. Despite all the corpses that had entered her life in the last year, she assumed the universe would act in her favor and her honeymoon would be off limits. But she'd been wrong before.

Ray and Ace stayed in the boat next to the body for the twenty minutes it took for uniformed officers to arrive on the scene. Autumn met them out front. With solemn expressions, they introduced themselves as officers Christine Campos and Alison Williams. Both wore their hair in tight buns. Officer Campos's brown skin and dark hair contrasted with her partner's fair skin and medium blonde hair. They came across as polite and capable. Autumn was glad to see female law enforcement officers and hoped that Ray would hire more in their hometown of Knollwood.

She and Chrissy escorted them to the lake and showed them to a canoe. The officers expertly maneuvered themselves into the boat despite the extensive array of weapons and accessories on their belts. Autumn was familiar with the stiff posture resulting from the heavy body armor under their shirts and was used to seeing the impressive way officers navigated the equipment that kept them safe.

The officers pulled their canoe next to Ray, and Autumn could read his lips, introducing himself as Lieutenant Reed and watched them shake hands. She heard car doors slamming at the front of the cabin and went to see who it was.

The Scranton crime scene investigation unit sent two investigators. A detective from Stroudsburg arrived right behind them in another vehicle. They walked with Autumn to the lake and assisted Ray and the officers to get the body to shore where a stretcher waited.

Autumn kept Chrissy away from the body to ensure her hair or other debris didn't contaminate any evidence. It was likely that the water probably did a good job of washing away most of the clues either way. They sat on the upper deck away from the water, watching the experts process the scene. Chrissy had seen her share of dead bodies, and Autumn wanted to spare her another one. It figures one would show up while they were on vacation.

The local officers, crime scene investigators, and the detective petted Ace and treated Ray with respect as they discussed how and when Ace discovered the bloated body. Officer Campos recognized the woman dressed in a red plaid flannel shirt and jeans as Loretta Armstrong, a server at The Tall Tree Inn. Loretta's feet were bare and toenails adorned with blue, sparkly polish to match her fingernails.

"She's been missing since last week," said officer Campos. "Her roommate, Cathy Bailey, described her clothing and nail polish when she made the report."

"Loretta Armstrong's mother reported her missing in Knollwood about a week ago. She disappeared after having dinner with friends at a local restaurant. How did she get all the way up here?" said Ray.

"She was driven or drove herself. We'll need to look for her car," said Officer Williams.

"It was a 2019 silver Corolla. Autumn found it about four miles from the restaurant where she was last seen," Ray offered. "If her roommate also reported her missing about the same time as Loretta's mother, Cathy Bailey has some explaining to do."

"We'll interview Ms. Bailey after the medical examiner's report is complete," said Detective John Conroy.

They promised to call Ray after the coroner examined the body. Ray knew a thorough exam would provide more details. Still, he knew the high likelihood that the water and aquatic wildlife inhabitants of the lake had destroyed important evidence.

"I'll contact my department and inform Detective Ross Adams. I believe Mr. and Mrs. Armstrong are staying at their house in Stroudsburg," said Ray, taking a card from Detective Conroy. "Will you be contacting them?"

Detective Conroy nodded somberly. There was nothing worse than notifying the family that their loved one was deceased.

Ray's mind raced with questions: How long had she been in the water? Did she drown, or was there another cause of death? Was it the result of foul play or accidental? So much for his vacation. He could still manage the investigation from here. No need to go back to Knollwood. Part of him wished their vacation was the tranquil, romantic respite they had planned. The other part of him felt more alive with a mystery to unravel. He'd do what he could to balance the situation and make it special for Autumn.

"Thanks, everyone," he said, shaking hands all around. "If anything else floats up, I'll let you know."

"Sure thing, Lieutenant," said Officer Campos. "In the meantime, we'll be combing the lake and surrounding areas for evidence."

He liked a powerful grip when shaking hands. Her firm handshake displayed confidence and authority. He knew how hard it was for female officers to come up through the ranks and earn acceptance by the men, especially women of color. Officer Williams had a solid grip as well. Ray observed them to be confident and formidable, traits he looked for in his officers back home.

Ray trudged up the wooden steps toward the upper deck. Autumn saw the concern in his eyes.

"It's Loretta," he said. "Detective Conroy is reaching out to Amy."

Autumn's eyes teared up. "Oh, no! Isn't the news better coming from us?"

"It's an official notification. Once she knows, you can reach out to her."

She stood, still holding Chrissy. He hugged them both and held her head against his chest.

"I'm sure Amy will call me after she's notified," Autumn sniffed, tears dotting Ray's T-shirt.

"Maybe being up here will help us get justice for Loretta."

Autumn nodded. "I hope so, though it would be little consolation for her family."

Chrissy squirmed to get down. She put Chrissy on the ground. She shook her long gray and white hair and pawed Ray's leg. He scooped her up.

"There's my little girl," he said, snuggling her.

"Let's explore some of the local spots and see what we can find out," said Autumn, wiping her tears and scanning the shoreline on the other side of the lake.

"See anything you like?" asked Ray, trying to lighten the moment.

"I'm thinking about Loretta. Could she have been visiting someone in one of these cottages? Maybe slipped on the dock, hit her head, and then fell into the water?"

"Anything is possible. Until we know more about her movements, it's hard to come up with a theory as to what happened."

Autumn nodded her agreement.

"Who's hungry?" she asked the pups. Their tails wagged enthusiastically.

"I am. I didn't get to finish breakfast," said Ray over a rumbling stomach.

The Tall Tree Inn allowed dogs, so the decision to go there was easy. A hostess led the four of them through the dining room and out onto the lovely deck overlooking a rushing creek. The dense green of the surrounding woods made the space feel intimate.

Autumn set water and food bowls under the table for Chrissy and Ace. Their noses explored the new environment before settling down for a cool drink of water. Ace gobbled his food while Chrissy picked at hers. They lay down on the blankets Autumn arranged on the floor and looked at the water, trees, and wildlife.

The server came over. Her short, black hair matched her short, black nails and showed off her multiple ear piercings.

"Hi, I'm Lily. I'll be taking care of you today."

"Hi, Lily," Autumn said with a smile.

"I see your furry kids have quite the set up. Let me know if they need anything."

"We appreciate that," said Ray.

They ordered raspberry ice teas and perused the menu, deciding what they wanted before the server returned with their drinks.

"We were talking about possibly buying a vacation home in this area," said Autumn. "Have you lived here long, Lily?"

"All my life. It was a great place to grow up. We have the Stroudfest in the fall. Great food. Live music. Tons of vendors. Lots of folks come and bring their dogs."

"Good to know. We're renting a lakefront house on Moonlight Lake. It's so peaceful there," said Ray.

"It was until this morning. I heard they found Loretta Armstrong's body floating in there."

Autumn and Ray looked at each other.

"How did you hear about that?" Ray asked, squinting at Lily.

"News travels fast around here. We were wondering when she would turn up."

"How long has she been missing?" asked Autumn.

"Loretta Armstrong works as a server here, or, er, did, but hasn't been at work for a week. She was visiting her mother."

"Were you close?" Ray queried.

"We've been working together for two years now."

"We're the ones who found the body. I'm Lieutenant Reed with the Knollwood police department," said Ray. "And this is my wife, Autumn."

Lily nodded, acknowledging both of them. Ray's title made her open up with more information.

"Her roommate, Cathy Bailey, came in here looking for her last week. We told her she was at her mom's house and she left. Didn't say goodbye, just walked out."

"Did you notice anything different about Loretta the last time you saw her?" asked Autumn.

Lily paused before she said, "Loretta was acting weird a couple of days before she went to her mom's."

"Weird how?" asked Autumn.

"She was moody, which isn't like her. Loretta usually made snarky comments, but she was quiet. Dark circles under her eyes. Something was wrong, but she didn't want to talk about it. Let me put your order in," she said, and walked away.

When Lily returned with their food, she said, "Enjoy your food. I hope you can relax at your cabin even after finding Loretta."

"Such an active grapevine here. We've become a part of it already. If we bought a vacation home here, they'll know us as the people who found the body," Autumn said, taking a bite of her grilled cheese, tomato, and bacon sandwich.

"That's how they know us at home, so we'd fit in quickly. I'm sure Chrissy can find even more bodies if we came up here more often."

Autumn's eyebrows went up. Ray smiled.

"Sorry. Just trying to keep it light." He took a bite of his Cuban sandwich piled with ham, Swiss, turkey, and pesto, wiping juice from his mouth. "At least we know the food is good."

"My eternal optimist." Autumn dabbed her napkin on a spot Ray missed.

"We need to find out what Loretta was upset about before she headed to Knollwood," said Autumn.

"Roger that," Ray answered, taking another bite of his sandwich.

⚡ 3 ⚡

The day was sunny and mild, perfect for a stroll around the lower portion of Moonlight Lake. A small bridge allowed visitors to cross at the narrowest part of the water between the upper and lower bodies of water. Ray pulled into the empty parking area of the nearest trailhead and grabbed the backpack from the SUV. Autumn had filled it with bottles of water for the four of them, portable bowls, poo bags, and snacks for the pups. Before lifting Chrissy out of her car seat, Autumn clipped a leash to her harness while Ray secured one to Ace's. Once on the ground, both pups shook out their fur and were ready for an adventure.

The smell of pine released into the air as they tromped over a bed of needles that lay on the well-worn path. Ace and Chrissy found a variety of interesting smells and stopped frequently to check them out and mark their spots.

Autumn clasped Ray's hand, happy for this beautiful day and being with her perfect little family. It was an odd mix of sorrow for Loretta's death and relief for being away from the responsibilities of running her bed-and-breakfast back home. The inn was in the capable hands of her cousin Beatrice Peabody and the inn's manager, Kim Stokes, who would call if there was a problem. All things considered; this was the most relaxed she'd been since before the wedding.

The trail twisted between the newly leafing trees.

"If we come up later in the year, we can see what this looks like in full leaf," said Ray.

"And the colors in the fall would be incredible."

"All the more reason to get an all-season cottage up here." Ray came to a quick stop when Ace discovered something he wanted to sniff under some brush.

Chrissy went to see what he found, but with less curiosity.

The water lapped against the bank of the lake, and Chrissy made a move toward the sound. Autumn waited to see if she'd try to wade in. Ace came over to Chrissy and nudged her away from the water.

Laughing, Autumn petted them both. "Let's go, kids."

Farther down the path, they saw a boat rental stand boasting flat bottom boats with electric motors, canoes, and kayaks. A man stood outside the booth, smiling.

"Hello," he said. "I am Miguel Lopez, owner of Moonlight Boat Rentals. Are you interested in cruising the lake today? We are a pet-friendly business."

"Good to know," said Ray, while petting Ace's head. "We have canoes at the house we're renting, but a flat-bottom boat could hold all of us."

"Very true!" said Miguel.

"We're Ray and Autumn Reed," Ray said and shook hands. "This little sweetheart is Chrissy and our noble guard dog is Ace."

"Ah, you're renting the house where they found Loretta!" said Miguel, nodding.

"I guess everyone in town knows by now," Autumn said, shaking her head.

"Oh, yes. Loretta rented a canoe from me the day before you found her, but she never came back here."

The lake Miguel's business was on was the same lake as the house Ray and Autumn rented, just in the lower half.

"How did she seem to you?" asked Ray.

"In a hurry. I couldn't launch the boat fast enough."

"Did she seem afraid?" asked Autumn, wondering why Loretta would be in such a hurry.

"Maybe. There were days when all she wanted to do was to be out on the lake and rushed me to get the boat in the water. But that day, she seemed more agitated than usual. Like someone was chasing her."

"Did you see anyone in the area? In the parking lot or on the trail? Or even on the lake?" asked Ray.

"No, but there was one odd thing."

"What's that?" asked Autumn. She hoped to get a morsel of useful information.

"I don't know how she got here. She didn't drive up like she usually does. Loretta's apartment is a few miles from here."

Ray and Autumn looked at each other, trying to process this information. The unspoken questions hung in the air: where did she come from and how did she get here?

"She never came back with my boat. The next day, I saw my canoe floating out there." Miguel pointed to the middle of the lake. "No one was in it, and it's still too cold to swim. I went out there with one of my flat bottom boats and towed it back in."

"So, you never heard from Loretta again," said Ray.

"No, and I was worried. She'd never leave my boat unattended."

"Did you report it to the police?" asked Autumn.

"I didn't know what happened. What could I report? I got my boat back, so it wasn't theft. And I didn't know she was officially missing until you found her body."

Autumn looked out over the lake, picturing the scene from Miguel's perspective. She understood his position, but looking over at Ray, he seemed skeptical.

"Do you live close by?" asked Autumn.

"This neighborhood is too expensive. I have an apartment about ten minutes away. Been there just over a year."

"How well did you know Loretta?" asked Ray.

"Just small conversations when she came to rent a boat. I'd see her sometimes when I went to Harley's General Store and she was working, but we didn't hang out or anything."

Miguel looked down the trail, seemingly glad for a diversion, and waved to two women who approached them.

"Amy!" Autumn ran up to Amy and hugged her. "We're so sorry for your loss," Autumn offered condolences. "We found her this morning. Actually, Ace spotted her."

Amy held onto Autumn, propping herself against her.

"For the life of me, I couldn't figure out where she could have gone. How did she make it all the way up here without her car?" Amy's voice trailed off, tears filling her eyes.

"You know she was unreliable, Mom. We didn't know where she was most of the time," snapped Madison.

"Autumn, this is my daughter, Madison."

Autumn held out her hand. "I'm sorry to meet you under these circumstances."

Madison didn't take her hand, but crossed her arms instead.

"Bobby usually knew where she was," Amy said, wiping her eyes.

"Bobby?" Autumn queried.

"Loretta's boyfriend, Bobby Ringbottom," Amy clarified.

"She didn't even contact him!" Madison insisted.

"How do you know? When did you speak to him?" Amy confronted her daughter accusingly.

Miguel stepped in. "How about a nice row on the lake to calm down? Free of charge?"

"I don't want to row on the lake where my daughter drowned!" Amy shouted and walked off.

Madison stared at her mother's back, shrugged, and half-heartedly waved goodbye as she left the others behind.

Chrissy and Ace began tugging on their leashes.

"That's our signal to get going," said Autumn.

"Does this trail loop back to the parking area?" Ray asked Miguel.

"Yes, take this fork and wind around to the left. I hope to see you again."

"I'm sure we will," said Autumn, leading the pups down the trail.

Ray waved at Miguel and caught up to Autumn, taking Ace's leash from her hand.

"What did you think of that exchange?" he asked.

Autumn crinkled her nose. "I think Madison knows more than she's letting on."

✄ 4 ✄

Obituary: Loretta Armstrong (1996-2024), East Stroudsburg, PA

Loretta Armstrong, 28, of East Stroudsburg, PA, worked as a server at The Tall Tree Inn in Stroudsburg and as a clerk at Harley's General Store. She loved making customers happy, spending time in the woods and canoeing, and enjoyed reading murder mysteries.

She leaves behind her parents, Amy and Barry Armstrong of Knollwood, PA, and her sister, Madison Armstrong, of East Stroudsburg, PA. A memorial service will take place on the beach at Moonlight Lake on May 12, 2024. We appreciate donations in Loretta's name to One Tree Planted*.

*One Tree Planted is a non-profit organization. Since 2014, they have planted over 135.5 million trees with 378 partners across 82 countries in North America, Latin America, Africa, Asia, Europe and the Pacific. For more information, go to OneTreePlanted.org.

Autumn, Ray, Chrissy, and Ace arrived at the lakeshore beach for Loretta's memorial service. They had donated to One Tree Planted, an organization that plants one tree for every dollar donated. From their contribution, the organization would plant a thousand trees in Loretta's name.

Chrissy walked tentatively, not sure if she liked the feel of sand on her paw pads. Autumn rescued her from the awkward footing, lifting her up and cradling her lovingly, kissing her head. Ace was bolder, charging down the dirt trail to the beach, pulling Ray behind him, and landing joyfully on the sand. Ray ruffled the thick fur on his head as his tongue lolled from exertion. A light breeze made Autumn glad she wore a black and cream cable-knit sweater with black jeans.

A group of about twenty-five people stood on the beach, floral wreaths stood in a U-shape around the mourners, and a podium stood over to the side. Autumn saw Amy standing with her daughter, Madison. She waved, but allowed the family space. Amy gave a slight nod in response. Miguel Lopez, Lily Harding, the server from the Tall Tree Inn, Detective John Conroy, and officers Christine Campos and Alison Williams, both dressed in uniform, stood nearby. A woman stood at the top of the bluff, arms crossed, observing the activity but making no move to participate in the service.

The officers came over and shook hands with Ray and Autumn and petted the fur babies. Detective Conroy stood next to Ray and spoke in hushed tones. Autumn heard Ray tell the three of them that Miguel had seen Loretta's rental canoe floating by itself the day before they found her. Alison wrote this information in her notebook and they promised to follow-up. Ray moved closer to Autumn and put his arm around her. She laced her fingers through the hand he had draped over her shoulder.

Casual dress of jeans, khakis, sweaters, and flannels adorned most mourners. A few more grievers arrived, including a man wearing a suit jacket. Alison told them his name was Harley Waters, owner of the general store where Loretta worked. She filled in a few more unfamiliar faces. Barry Armstrong, Loretta's father, stood next to his wife, Amy. Bobby Ringbottom, Loretta's boyfriend, consoled Madison with his arm around her.

The roommate who reported Loretta missing, Cathy Bailey, sat on a rock, swaying back and forth, wringing her hands. She occasionally looked at the woman overlooking the ceremony and made eye contact and frowned, but didn't wave. The local dog groomer, Kirby Galloway, dabbed her eyes as she stood next to Cathy, patting her shoulder. Finally, Danny Cole, a bartender at the Log Cabin Bar, stood alone, with his arms crossed and a scowl on his face.

There were others from the area, but the officers couldn't identify them.

The lack of sorrow among attendees surprised Autumn. They seemed like they had some place else they needed to be and this was an inconvenience. The last funeral she had attended was for her parents. There were hundreds of people there, tears flowing, including her own. She smelled like fifty scents of perfume from people hugging her. Thinking about it made her tear up even now. Poor Loretta. Her departure deserved more emotion from the mourners. Autumn watched Amy, so composed with an undertone of sadness. Barry was stoic. Their reaction astonished Autumn. They had lost a child, after all.

Harley looked over at Cathy and followed her gaze to the hill, where the woman paced back and forth, fists clenched. She saw she had his attention and stopped, staring him down. He looked away.

Amy Armstrong went up to the podium and thanked everyone for coming. "Thank you for honoring Loretta by joining us today. We'd like you to share your cheerful stories of our daughter. She loved to laugh. The lake and the trees brought her the greatest joy. And then came her devotion to family and friends. I'm opening the floor to anyone who'd like to share a memory of Loretta."

Lily, Kirby, and Danny rolled their eyes and pursed their lips. What did the three of them know about Loretta that made them react so disrespectfully?

Harley Waters came up to the podium, glancing at the woman on the bluff as he walked. Her hands were on her hips. He took off his baseball cap, sporting a patch with a logo that said Harley's General Store over a picture of trees bordering a lake.

"As most of you know, Loretta worked for me at the general store. She could be moody, if truth be told."

The mourners chuckled.

"When she was on her game, she came up with good ideas for displays and organizing the store. In my mind, I keep seeing her sweeping the floor and drinking all my Redbulls without paying."

Another quiet laugh swept through the crowd.

"I'll miss her quirkiness and unpredictability," Harley finished, donned his cap, and rejoined the group.

Cathy Bailey spoke next.

"After a week without Loretta in the apartment, I realized how noisy she was. And also, messy. Her stuff is still all over her room and most of our chairs have clothes draped over them. There's still the smell of bacon in the kitchen. That was her favorite food. But the place feels empty. I keep waiting for her to walk in the door so we can fight about cleaning up. It's up to me now. Anybody looking for a place to stay, let me know."

The lack of the words *I'll miss her* or *I loved her* struck Autumn. So far, memories included Loretta being a slob, having a moody disposition, and stealing from the general store owner. Knowing the deceased seemed like a chore based on what these folks had to say.

Miguel Lopez was up next.

"Loretta came to my place often to rent canoes. I tried treating her right, sometimes giving her a discount. She always seemed to be in a hurry to get out on the lake, but once she launched the boat, she paddled slowly, sometimes putting the oar in her lap and looking around. I had a bad feeling the day I saw her canoe floating on the lake without her. It was strange thinking that I'd never see her again."

Miguel's statement said he knew he'd never see her again puzzled Autumn. He told them he wasn't sure what happened; hence, he didn't report it to the police. She looked over at Ray, who had the frown he got when he spotted a lie.

Autumn noticed Madison and Bobby whispering frantically, eyebrows drawn together, fists clenched. Chrissy was getting heavy, so she put her down gently. The Shih Tzu, ever curious, went over to where they were arguing and looked up at the pair. They looked down at the fluffy dog and stopped to shoo her away. She ran back to Autumn, who kneeled down and put her head against Chrissy's. Touching her forehead to Chrissy's head made the world spin backwards and then cleared to show Madison's cardigan open and a bump on her belly under the T-shirt she wore. It looked like Madison was pregnant from this angle and hard to tell from a frontal view.

After Autumn adopted the Shih Tzu, she discovered Chrissy had a special telepathic ability to show her mommy what she witnessed. It was always from the visual perspective of Chrissy's eye level, so it was an optical adjustment that was sometimes accompanied by nausea. Ray was the only other person with whom she shared her unique talent. It had helped solve crimes, giving Autumn and Ray information they would not otherwise have. They had told no one else; Chrissy was their secret weapon. People didn't suspect that Chrissy could share what she saw, so they thought nothing of her presence and behaved with impunity.

They waited, but no one else came up to speak, so Amy guided each person to take a pink carnation bud and set it afloat on the water to signify never forgetting the departed. As the pink flowers floated off into Moonlight Lake, there were no tears, and Kirby Galloway had stopped dabbing her eyes. The mourners trudged up the trail, leaving Ray, Autumn, John, Christine, and Alison to chat.

"That was a strange memorial service," said Autumn, setting Chrissy on the sand.

"You know these folks best. Did this seem like behavior you'd expect from them?" asked Ray as he unhooked Ace and Chrissy from their harnesses. Autumn watched the two of them run side-by-side a little way down the beach, exploring the shoreline.

"Good thing we brought the protective covers for the SUV. There's going to be sand everywhere," Autumn thought aloud.

Alison laughed. "But they're fun to watch. I love dogs."

Christine smiled and nodded her head in agreement.

"When we questioned the family, they seemed oddly unaffected by Loretta's disappearance, as though it wasn't unusual for her to take off," said Detective John Conroy.

"Lily at the Tall Trees restaurant said she skipped work a lot, but didn't know where she went. Her roommate, Cathy, said her frequent absence created the mess they lived in. And Harley at the General Store didn't miss her if she didn't show, because then nothing got stolen. Occasionally, he found money missing, besides losing out from Loretta's Redbull habit. Seems like it was easier when she wasn't around," summarized Christine.

"They all admitted their issues with her during the service, like it was common knowledge," Alison said.

"Did you notice her sister Madison is pregnant?" asked Autumn, careful not to include Chrissy as the source of that information.

"Hmm. I saw her arguing with Bobby Ringbottom during the gathering. That means they're close enough to have something to fight about," observed Alison.

Ray nodded. "I find it odd that her father, sister, nor boyfriend had anything to say on her behalf."

"I'd say it's hard to speak about a departed loved one without breaking down in front of people, but they didn't look bereaved," Autumn said.

"Who was the woman on the bluff?" asked Ray.

Detective Conroy responded. "Monica Bailey, Cathy's mother. A bitter, controlling woman. Never has anything nice to say and constantly berates Cathy in front of others. People steer clear of her."

"I wonder why she didn't come down to the beach," said Autumn.

"We'll see what we can find out," said John. Alison and Christine nodded. They shook hands and left the beach.

Ray and Autumn let the pups play for a while before heading back to the rental home.

5

Autumn and Ray lounged in bed after a passionate morning celebrating in true honeymoon fashion, until Ace and Chrissy had finished napping and took a running leap onto the bed. They laughed at their pawing and lying on their backs for belly rubs, demanding attention as though deprived. When the activity settled down to snuggles all around, they realized it was dinnertime.

"Let's go out for dinner," Autumn suggested. "How about the Log Cabin Bar?"

Ray chuckled. "And maybe we'll run into Danny Cole, if we're lucky?"

Autumn flushed and gave him a lopsided smile.

"To be honest, I was thinking the same thing."

"They have an outdoor dining area and pub food."

After showering and packing the pups' to-go bag containing their bowls, snacks, and dinner, Ray called, "C'mon, kids. Get in the car!"

Chrissy and Ace dropped the toys they were playing with and charged to the door. Ray got them in the car and brought their harnesses and leashes. Autumn grabbed their cushions. They drove for ten minutes to get to the restaurant.

The building was not surprisingly a rustic log cabin, hence the name. They drove around to find a parking space in the crowded lot. A patio with an awning had tables overlooking the lake. The water sparkled in the late-day sunlight as boaters glided lazily between the red and white striped buoy markers. The steps leading to the outdoor patio had a hostess podium with a friendly woman ready to attend to them. Her name tag said Barbara.

"Party of four," Ray said with a wide smile.

Barbara got the joke and returned his smile. "Right this way," she said, grabbing two menus. "We have a doggy special today. Ground meat with no bun, flavorings, or spices, mixed with egg and plain breadcrumbs."

Autumn positioned the pups' cushions to be out of the way of the server and other guests, along with their bowls. "They might like that. We can put it with their kibble."

"Enjoy," said Barbara, putting down their menus and walking away.

They ordered drinks and burgers all around, two doggy specials, a burger with tomato and avocado for Autumn, and one with bacon and cheese for Ray. They looked out over the lake.

"I haven't been this relaxed in a long time," said Ray, reaching out to hold her hand across the table.

Autumn noticed his breathing was deeper than usual. Normally, he seemed to breathe at the base of his throat, stress inhibiting a large intake of air.

"It's beautiful here, and calm, mostly. There's still a murder to solve."

"Maybe I'll take a walk to the men's room. It's just past the bar, isn't it?" He winked at Autumn and went inside the dark bar.

Ray waited a moment for his eyes to adjust from the evening sunlight to the dim inside lighting. Behind the long wooden bar, he saw Danny Cole, waiting on customers. A few stools were open, and Ray took a seat toward the end of the counter. Danny came over, wiping the veined granite surface as he moved.

"What can I get you?" asked Danny.

"Whatever's on tap, thanks."

Danny poured the beer into a chilled glass and set it in front of Ray on a coaster. The perfect pour impressed Ray.

"I saw you at the memorial service, didn't I?" asked Ray, then took a sip of his ice-cold beer.

"Oh, yeah. I thought you looked familiar. The one with the dogs, right?"

"Yep. They come with us everywhere. They're out on the patio right now."

"So, why are you in here?" Danny asked suspiciously.

"I ordered iced tea with dinner and decided to grab a beer, too, without bothering our server."

Danny nodded, looking at Ray with a sideways glance.

"How do you know Loretta?"

"She floated up to our dock. Sad thing. Such a young girl." He took another sip of beer, not wanting to give away the fact that they knew Loretta's mother.

"Weird that she drowned. She and I got our lifesaving certificates the same summer."

"She spent a lot of time on the water?"

"Yeah, swimming and canoeing. The rest of the time, she used to come in here a lot after work or when she'd skip work."

"Were you close?"

"I tried to be, but it was hard when she made fun of me; my cowlick, the way I say certain words, my job."

"Like in grade school, sometimes the one who likes you the most teases you."

"I don't know. She had a boyfriend and made mean comments to others, but mostly to me. She could be nasty to people. I liked her a lot, even though she embarrassed me. It's not the way to have a good relationship. That's why I didn't speak at the memorial service. I couldn't think of anything nice to say."

"That didn't stop those who spoke about her. Death has a way of making us take a second look at ourselves and relationships. It makes things raw and forces us to question the way we feel about the deceased. Sometimes people get so emotional it overrides their sense of logic. They lose control and lash out. Any idea who might have been angry enough to kill her?"

Danny's face dropped. "I, I don't know. The three people closest to her were Madison, Bobby, and Cathy. Maybe they can help you."

Ray swigged the rest of his beer. "Thanks, Danny. I better get back to my table. Nice chatting with you." Ray tossed some money on the counter, enough for the beer and an abundant tip.

Danny waved; Ray saw his eyes widen when he saw the amount of the tip.

"There you are!" said Autumn.

"I was talking to Danny Cole. He said Loretta was nasty to him and to others and pointed to Madison, Bobby, and Cathy. One of those people may have reached their limit."

The server came over with their food. After filling Chrissy and Ace's bowls, they dug in to their own food.

6

Ray called Detective Ross Adams in Knollwood to see what progress he'd made in questioning the friends who had seen Loretta for dinner before her disappearance.

"Hey, Ross. How are things in Knollwood?"

"Aren't you supposed to be on your honeymoon? I've got the investigation at this end."

"Yeah, well, things are progressing somewhat here, but I need whatever you found out from Loretta's dinner companions and the car." Ray briefed Ross on what had transpired in Stroudsburg.

"Sounds like there's no shortage of suspects where you are, that's for sure. First, the car. It was out of gas. We looked up Loretta's cell phone records, and there wasn't a call to roadside assistance or a gas station. We also found a gas station receipt on the floor of her car that showed she filled her tank the day before she had dinner with friends."

"No wonder she started heading up to the mountains without checking her gas gauge. She thought she had plenty of gas. But why not call for help? We know she had her phone based on eyewitnesses at the River Café."

"I thought the same thing," confirmed Ross. "She didn't even go back to her mom's house to pick up any personal items she had traveled with. Loretta headed north right out of the restaurant."

"Then how did she get all the way up here without her car or calling anyone for a ride?"

"That's the million-dollar question!" Ross continued. "The friends here had a consistent story. That Loretta was visiting her mother for a few days and they got together for dinner. They hadn't seen her in a while. She was upset by a call from her boyfriend, Bobby Ringbottom, saying he needed to see her right away, but he didn't tell her why."

"The hostess at the restaurant told Autumn that Loretta didn't plan to go back to Stroudsburg for a few days, so why was her car heading in that direction rather than back to her mother's place?"

"Her friends said the same thing. What would make her change her mind? Curiosity? Upset? Maybe she didn't call her mother because it was too late and didn't want to wake her?" offered Detective Adams.

"The change in plans surprised them just as much as it surprised us."

"Yep. And then a couple of them told me how she'd been fighting with Bobby. Getting away from him was the purpose of the trip to Knollwood."

"But none of them knew what they were fighting about?"

"Loretta confided in a woman named Jane Roscoe, and told her it was about her sister, Madison. She'd been hanging out with Loretta and Bobby too much and flirting with him."

"That makes sense. Madison and Bobby were arguing at Loretta's memorial service, and Madison may be pregnant. I'll work that angle from up here. Was there any security camera footage from outside the restaurant?"

"Nope, no cameras."

"That's frustrating. Keep me posted on anything else that comes up."

"Whatever you need. Remember, you're on vacation."

Ray heard Ross chuckle, knowing he couldn't help but pursue the investigation, honeymoon or not.

Autumn sipped a cup of herbal tea with Chrissy seated next to her on the couch across from Amy Armstrong. Inviting Amy over to their rental house was long overdue. Autumn knew what it was like to lose loved ones, but couldn't imagine losing a child.

Dark circles stood out under Amy's eyes despite the bright sunlight streaming in through floor-to-ceiling lake view windows. Amy's misery prevented her from enjoying the beauty of the scenery.

"Can you think of anyone who would want to harm Loretta?" asked Autumn as gently as she could.

"Loretta fought with everyone, including me. I tried to emphasize how important it was to have good relationships. She told me I didn't know anything about life." Amy took a sip of tea.

"Did anyone ever threaten her or did she threaten to hurt anyone?" Autumn bit into a sugar cookie.

"She complained a lot about her roommate. How she was always pushing her to clean up the apartment. Sadly, I admit she was a slob."

"What about her boyfriend, Bobby? How were they getting along?"

Amy grunted. "On and off. Loretta thought he was cheating on her. He said he wasn't. Who knows what the truth is? I was just hoping she'd get frustrated enough to get him out of her life. He's one of those guys that depends on his youthful good looks, not realizing it doesn't last forever. His ego got fed every time a woman flirted with him. I know Loretta was tired of him paying attention to other women, especially when she was with him."

"What does your gut tell you about Loretta's death?"

"Depression won; she gave up, and let herself drown in her beloved lake." Amy's head lowered, but no tears came.

"You think she committed suicide?" Autumn found this a strange conclusion, given what they knew so far. "I heard she had a lifesaving certification."

"Uh, well, uh, I don't know what to make of her death," Amy stumbled over her words.

"What did you think happened when you called me after she disappeared? Were you worried that she was suicidal?"

"Listen, I have nothing more to say about this situation. I just lost my daughter and don't want to talk about it anymore. Thanks for the tea."

Amy gathered herself and headed for the front door. Autumn walked her out, neither saying a word.

Closing the door behind Amy, Autumn wondered what she was hiding.

7

Amy watched the ground as she made her way to the car parked in front of Autumn's rental house. To cut Autumn off like that was rude. After all, she was only trying to help. Maybe it was a bad idea to involve her when Loretta disappeared. Either way, Loretta had found her way to Autumn and Ray. With their track record of solving murders, she hoped justice would come to her daughter.

So, what made her so tense about this situation? Yes, she grieved her daughter despite the rocky relationship they had, but worried if there was more to lose once the police solved the case. And what of her relationship with Barry? They'd been married almost thirty years and the secrets she held close might break them apart if they ever got out.

Barry had his own struggles with the loss of Loretta. She stole money from his wallet several times and was more tolerant than Amy thought he should be, but he was one to harbor his thoughts and feelings for periods of time and then explode over minor incidents.

As she turned the key in the ignition, Amy worried about her remaining family members and how Loretta's death would affect their relationships. She was already arguing with Madison, who was more belligerent than usual. The jealousy and resentment Madison had toward Loretta should have died with Loretta, but she continued to lash out. Maybe it was guilt, or regret that she hadn't resolved their issues before her sister died.

In all the years they'd been coming up here, Loretta loved it the most. She preferred the woods and the lake to crowds and traffic. But even up here, she didn't get along with people. Her death on Moonlight Lake was tragic, yet appropriate, since she loved it so much. Amy wondered, if she were on the lake alone, how did she die? She was an excellent swimmer, and Miguel didn't see anyone else out there, at least on his portion of the lake. He couldn't see past the curvature of the shoreline that led to the part where Autumn and Ray were staying. Maybe the autopsy would provide some answers.

Madison Armstrong was uncomfortable on the hard bench in front of Harley's General Store. Her belly was growing and adding weight to her normally slender frame. This wasn't the plan. She hadn't wanted to get pregnant and didn't know how she'd afford to raise a child once it came into the world. The baby's daddy had no interest in being a father or using his money to support it.

Out in front of Loretta's secondary workplace, Madison almost expected her sister to run up the front steps, late as usual, for her shift. She never understood Loretta, how she could have two jobs and no money, how she knew lots of people but sabotaged all of her relationships, and how she enjoyed throwing her relationship with Bobby in Madison's face. He was the best-looking guy in town and most women his age made a play for him. It puzzled her how Loretta landed him, even though she was prettier than Madison, striking, mysterious. She strutted her perfect figure like a peacock whenever Madison was around. But she had a nasty disposition, and Bobby had a roving eye.

They were only two years apart and had some mutual friends, but neither invited the other out for drinks or dinner with those in their respective circles. Nor did they get together, just the two of them. It appeared they weren't sisters at all. Some people commented on how they didn't resemble each other like you'd expect.

Sharing news of the pregnancy was out of the question. She hadn't even told her parents. Barely showing at two months, she figured no one would know for another couple of months. Not sure how her parents would react, she sat on the information, especially since they just lost Loretta. She didn't want to overwhelm them.

Madison wondered how many people suspected her of killing Loretta, knowing how they didn't get along and Madison's constant complaining to anyone who would listen. She'd planned it in her head many times, thinking that the world, or at least Madison's world, would be better without her sister in it. Now that she was gone, things weren't that much different. Her fantasy was better than the reality. Most people didn't comment on their relationship; it was a given that the two didn't get along. It had been like that since childhood. The folks living in the mountains were more aware of it than those in Knollwood.

Harley came out of the store, interrupting her thoughts.

"Hey, Madison. How are you holding up?"

"Okay, I guess."

"Want something cold to drink? I can go grab it out of the fridge."

"No, thanks. I was just sitting here thinking about Loretta. The place still has her imprint on it."

"That it does. It's strange knowing she'll never be back here."

Madison nodded. "I'm going for a walk. See ya, Harley."

"Take care."

Madison walked a little way down the road to the trailhead leading back toward her mother's house. Harley was the nicest guy she ever met and couldn't understand how Loretta could take advantage of him. She breathed deeply as she walked, hoping it would clear the anxiety building in her gut. Alone on the trail, she jumped a little when she heard a twig snap. Figuring it must be an animal, she kept going, stretching her arms as she walked. A squirrel skittered across the trail and up a tree. She visualized life without Loretta and felt relieved at the idea. No more fighting. No more competition. Things would get better.

Rustling in the bushes made her stop and look. A doe peered over the foliage. She was chewing something. The deer startled and took off into the forest.

That's when a person appeared out of the woods, grinning.

"I didn't expect to see you today," said Madison.

They didn't reply, but took a long-bladed dagger and, with a swish, Madison fell to the ground.

≈ 8 ≈

Ray came in looking tired. He petted Chrissy and Ace as he made his way to Autumn. Wrapping his arms around her, he squeezed her tight and kissed her.

"Sorry that took so long," he said.

"You're just in time. I made dinner. The pups already ate. Let's just have a romantic night in."

He nodded and went over to the sink to wash his hands before sitting down at the table. Autumn positioned his place setting so that he faced the lake. She brought over the food, filled his glass with lemonade, and heard him sigh as the view helped him decompress. While she wished she had him to herself on their honeymoon, Autumn appreciated the effort of making the most of their time together.

"Loretta didn't drown," said Ray, as he took a forkful of pasta.

Autumn waited. Ray looked into her eyes.

"Someone stabbed her. She was dead before being dumped in the lake. There was no water in her lungs."

Autumn's face crinkled up, incredulous at the news.

"The medical examiner gave us an idea of the shape of the weapon. It's a slender dagger with a seven-inch blade."

"Has Amy been told, yet?"

"Detective Conroy is notifying her now."

Autumn put down her fork, shaking her head.

"Where's the crime scene? There was no blood in the car when I peeked through the window. And, even before that, how did she get all the way up to the mountains without her car?"

"The questions keep piling up. We're looking for answers," Ray assured her.

Chrissy appeared next to Autumn, waiting for a lift onto her mommy's lap.

"How do you always know when I need snuggles, little one?"

Ray took another bite of his dinner and a sip of water.

"Loretta had been in the water for a couple of days, according to the medical examiner. That means we have no trace evidence from her attacker, like fingerprints or DNA."

"So, when Amy reported her missing, she was likely already dead or killed shortly after."

"Correct," confirmed Ray.

"Is it possible that Amy reported her missing from Knollwood as a distraction? Is she involved?"

Ray shrugged. "For that matter, Cathy Bailey also reported her missing from East Stroudsburg. That's stranger than Amy Armstrong worried about her daughter. We have lots to sort out."

"She was acting weird when I had her over for tea, like she was hiding something. I don't know what it could be, but she seemed afraid of going too deep into sharing information."

Ray took a bite of garlic bread. A murder case didn't affect his appetite. "The woman stayed very much on the surface of who Loretta was at the memorial service. I'm not surprised she didn't open up to you under questioning."

"I didn't question her!"

Ray's eyebrows went up.

"Okay, maybe I was on a fact-finding mission. I hoped there were clues in what Amy could share; information she didn't realize might be important."

"I know how your mind works." He reached for her hand and stroked it. "Your intentions are good and your motivation is to solve the case. I get it."

"That's right. So why did she get mad and abruptly leave?"

Ray wiped his mouth. "I can't determine that based on what we know. Amy may have been scared of telling you too much. After all, you're married to a law enforcement officer."

Autumn gave him a gleaming smile. "That I am." She brought his hand to her mouth and kissed it lovingly.

"Now, what movie did you want to watch?"

"I'll find one while you pour the wine."

The next morning, Autumn, Ray, Chrissy, and Ace woke from a good night's sleep in the king-size bed positioned next to a massive window overlooking the lake. It was a serene way to wake up. Ace was reluctant to move, comfortably stretched out on his side at Ray's feet. Chrissy snuggled between Ray and Autumn, lying on her back, contentedly getting a belly rub from her mommy.

"I love these lazy mornings," said Autumn.

"Me, too," Ray said and pulled her toward him for a kiss.

"I could get used to this as a vacation spot. Maureen could find us the perfect place."

Maureen Roberts was the Clarke family friend and realtor for decades. Sometimes it was odd for Autumn to refer to herself as Autumn Reed instead of Clarke, but every time she looked at Ray, she knew she'd made the right decision.

"I'm in," Ray agreed.

"We have enough eggs and food for all of us to have breakfast, but we need to make a trip to Harley's General Store for supplies."

"I'll shower and get cooking."

"And I'll let the pups out." Autumn threw back the blankets. "Come on!" she called to Chrissy and Ace, who leaped off the bed and did zoomies through the house until they reached the back door. She pulled back the sliding door, and they charged down the porch steps to the grassy patches close to the lake. The fenced yard made it easy to let them out, as long as they didn't decide to jump in the water.

They ran inside, and Autumn filled their water bowls and poured kibble in their bowls. Ray would add scrambled eggs to the kibble. He used water instead of milk to make them fluffy. He said that's what chefs do. Autumn didn't know if that was true, but his scrambled eggs were the best, so she didn't question it.

Fed, showered, and packed up, they jumped in the SUV and headed to Harley's. On the way, they passed a trailhead perfect to take Chrissy and Ace on a new adventure before shopping. They varied the sections of woods where they walked here and at home to enhance the sights and smells for the furry kids to explore.

The parking area was empty, so they looked forward to a quiet walk without excessive foot traffic. Leashes on, they headed into the woods. A couple of deer stared at them. Ace barked, scaring them, and they leaped through the brush to get away.

"Hey, buddy, that wasn't nice," Ray calmly scolded him.

Ace wagged his tail.

Chrissy was trying to figure out what the commotion was about and decided it wasn't worth the trouble, so she kept walking. A chipmunk ran across the trail, and that's when Chrissy tried charging after it, barking, stopped by the leash.

"Okay, my little huntress," Autumn chuckled, pulling her back into step.

The trail curved. Ace picked up a scent and put his nose to the ground, dragging Ray with him. Autumn picked up Chrissy so they could keep up. About fifty yards down the trail, Ace sat and stared at the body of Madison Armstrong.

Ray felt for a pulse that he'd never find. He called Detective Conroy.

Officers Campos and Williams arrived ahead of Detective Conroy to secure the scene. Autumn took the pups back to their vehicle and waited while law enforcement did their thing. When Alison emerged from the woods, she approached Autumn.

"Not much of a honeymoon, is it?"

Autumn slowly shook her head. "We have the rest of our lives together. Poor Amy lost two daughters within a week. How will she survive this?"

Alison pressed her lips together. It was hard on everyone when someone died, especially if it involved murder.

"Ace is quite a tracker. Who knows how long it would've been if he hadn't found her?"

"Yes, he's a retired officer, but his training stays with him. Even Chrissy finds bodies. Between the two of them, nothing goes unnoticed."

Alison nodded.

The medical examiner's team emerged from the trail wheeling a gurney with a body bag on top, followed by Ray Reed, Christine Campos, and John Conroy, all wearing grim expressions. Down the road, they saw Harley Waters watching the activity. He waved.

"I'll go talk to him," said Detective Conroy. "Maybe he saw something that could help."

The officers waited for the crime scene techs to show up. Ray got into their SUV and slammed the door closed.

"Stabbed with a dagger similar to the one that killed Loretta," he said.

"It's likely the same killer, then," said Autumn.

"That's the prevailing theory. Let's go get supplies and head back to the house."

Ray stayed outside with the pups, John Conroy, and Harley Waters, while Autumn went into the general store. She bought eggs, bacon, bread, coffee, a jug of iced tea, dog snacks, popcorn, and ice cream. A clerk rang her up. When she came out, the three men were still talking. Ray saw her and excused himself.

"Thanks for the information, Harley. I'll be talking to you, John."

Ray got in the car and told Autumn about Harley talking to Madison before she walked into the woods. That was yesterday, late afternoon. "She's been in the woods overnight. Good thing we found her before animals started destroying evidence."

"I guess Detective Conroy will speak to Amy. I'll wait for her to reach out to me. After the way she left the other day, I don't want to antagonize her."

"With all this craziness, how about we watch a movie at the house and just relax? We can order dinner. I'll even give you a massage."

"Sounds great. I bought popcorn and ice cream, so we're all set."

9

The news of Madison's murder reverberated through the community and landed squarely on Bobby Ringbottom's head. As much as they argued, he'd miss Madison. It took a lot of convincing for her to believe that Bobby no longer had feelings for Loretta, and she never completely believed it until her sister was dead. Even at that, she still brought it up at their most intimate moments.

He was tired of her paranoia and jealousy and hoped she'd change, but even though the circumstances put the two of them in a better position to be together, Madison's suspicious nature persisted. The pregnancy made it worse. It was infuriating. And now she was gone. Somehow, he felt lighter than when she was around. They had chemistry, physically, anyway, but outside of that, they were incompatible.

Having been with both sisters, he concluded they were each a problem in their own way. He fought with them about different things, but it amounted to the same level of frustration. Bobby wanted out, and neither would let him go.

He had his eye on Lily Harding and frequently had lunch at the Tall Tree Inn when she was working. Loretta thought he came to see her, but he'd watch Lily bustling about waiting tables in her form-fitting black uniform. Sometimes, Loretta caught him looking, and a fight would ensue. The boss didn't like it and Lily stayed out of it, but Bobby could tell she enjoyed the attention. She'd look over to see if he was watching her. When he'd wink at her, a beautiful smile broke across her face, making him want her more.

Besides, he'd seen Danny Cole from the Log Cabin Bar checking out Loretta and her flirting back. She pretended not to like him in front of Bobby and wasn't sure if she was actually interested in Danny. He began hoping they'd start something so he could exit the relationship. It never happened as far as he knew.

He had his eye on Lily at Loretta's memorial service. She felt his gaze on her and acknowledged it with a demure return glance, which led to an argument with Madison. It wasn't something he wanted to relive. Loretta was gone and that should have ended it. But Madison was more like Loretta than she realized. She betrayed Loretta in so

many ways that even though Bobby was in on it, he didn't trust her.
And now he was free of them both.

Ray planned to meet with Detective Conroy that afternoon, so
Autumn called Kirby Galloway to see if she could do an in-home
grooming appointment for Chrissy and Ace. They were gamey from
the walks in the woods and the sandy lakeshore. The unspoken
connection with Chrissy let her know that her fur baby preferred her
hair clean and coiffed to tangled and smelly. Although Autumn
brushed her regularly, it wasn't the same as a professional grooming
appointment. Ace's dense fur also needed attention.

Kirby was available and happy to come to their cabin to service
the pups. She brought a portable grooming table big enough for Ace's
comfort and safety, a professional blow dryer, and all the tools of the
trade. All except shampoo. Autumn insisted on their usual organic
shampoo and brought it with them on the trip.

Kirby took the time to get to know the two fur babies, saying it's
easier to groom dogs after establishing a rapport. She threw balls,
played tug of war with their toys, and massaged them, chatting with
Autumn the whole time. It seemed she was also good at building trust
with pet parents.

She set-up the table and brushed out Ace first. Clumps of hair
came from his undercoat. He seemed to enjoy the deep brushing and
cooperated during the bathing and drying portion of the groom.
When finished, he walked over to his bed and fell asleep.

It was Chrissy's turn. They discussed a teddy bear cut and keeping
her hair long enough for a topknot. Kirby got to work brushing
Chrissy while letting Autumn in on local gossip.

"It's a real shame about Loretta," said Kirby.

"Yes, it is. How long have you known her?" asked Autumn.

"My whole life. I'm about ten years older than Loretta. I
remember when she was born. It caused quite a stir."

"What do you mean?"

"Most people knew about Amy and Harley being together. She
met him when she and Barry bought a vacation house up here.
Harley is easy to like. He's such a great guy. People could see she was
hot for Harley, but something happened between them and they
called it quits, but not before she got pregnant with Loretta."

"I had no idea," said Autumn, startled by the news.

"Neither did Barry. I'm not sure he ever knew, but the sisters look very different from one another. He'd be blind not to see it."

"Sometimes people don't want to see what's right in front of them."

"You can tell Madison is his, uh, er, was fathered by Barry."

Kirby paused and took a breath.

"Did Madison know Loretta was her half-sister?"

"I'm not sure. They fought constantly, always competing with one another. If Madison knew, she said nothing to me about it. Who knows if that information would make their arguments more intense or not?"

"Is that why Barry didn't speak at Loretta's service?"

"Probably. Maybe he figured it out and felt embarrassed. He's a quiet guy who keeps to himself no matter what. I know he avoids Harley's General Store. Drives out of his way to get eggs and such. But Amy still goes in."

"They've been married for over twenty years. To keep a secret that long takes some doing," Autumn said.

"Amy kept it to herself; it was others who talked about the way they looked at each other. Barry just wasn't part of those circles."

Autumn nodded. Her questions on the day Amy came over had gotten too close to her long-held secret. No wonder Amy got so defensive last time she was here. Rather than lie, she left.

"You said you don't want a summer cut, right?"

"Keep her at least two to three inches long on the body and longer on her head for a topknot. She's got a wardrobe of stylish bows I want her to wear."

"Okey-dokey. Let's wash you, little one!"

Kirby lifted Chrissy and took her to the tub. She brought her back wrapped in two towels, with her sweet, wet face sticking out. Autumn gave her a kiss before Kirby put her on the grooming table.

"I didn't really know Loretta. I'm closer to Amy. Do you think the comments people made at the memorial service were accurate?"

"Oh, yes. It shocked me that Miguel said anything at all, especially after Loretta gave him a one-star review for his business."

"She was there a lot, according to Miguel, and he treated her well. Why would she do that?"

"He didn't tolerate her mean comments about the condition of his boats and the prices he charged. His business is seasonal, so, of course, it'll be more expensive."

"True."

"One day, he tried explaining that to her, and that night, she wrote a scathing review that cut his business by half."

"That's terrible!"

"Yep." The conversation paused as Kirby flipped on the blow dryer until Chrissy's hair was dry and fluffy, and then snipped Chrissy's bangs carefully and shaped the hair on her face.

"It seems like she created conflict with everyone she met."

"That's Loretta!"

"Her boyfriend didn't speak at the service, either."

"Nope. He was actually seeing Madison before Loretta went to visit her mom. Madison told me she planned to take Bobby away from her sister."

"Nice." Autumn didn't know how to respond to the extensive family drama. If she had a sister, she couldn't imagine hurting her by stealing someone she loved.

"Loretta had her suspicions and was thinking about breaking up with Bobby. She knew how much Danny liked her and thought she'd try to have a relationship with him. Besides, she didn't like Bobby's dagger collection. It made her nervous."

Both girls stabbed, and Bobby connected to both. She felt her jaw clench with tension.

"Who do you think could have killed Loretta and Madison? Could it have been the same person?"

"Maybe, and there's one more person with a motive to end Loretta's life. Her roommate, Cathy. Loretta blackmailed her, threatening to tell her boss about her head injury. She wasn't able to perform her job like she used to, so she'd bring work home and Loretta would help her with spreadsheets and stuff. The woman had skills even though she was lazy."

"What did Loretta get from the blackmail?"

"Free rent."

Autumn thought about this. It's no wonder Loretta didn't feel compelled to show up for work. She lived for free.

"Cathy's mother, Monica Bailey, may have had a hand in it, too. She pushed Cathy to stop the blackmail by ending Loretta's life."

Autumn shook her head. Her own mother would never suggest such a thing or carry out a threat like that.

"Do you think Monica would commit the crime herself?"

"Hard to say. She has a history of lashing out. I think That's probably why she was pacing at the top of the bluff during the memorial service."

"That was Cathy's mother? I saw her looking up at her, but didn't know why."

"Yup!"

Kirby combed Chrissy's face one last time, pulled her hair into a topknot with a coated rubber band, and plucked a pink satin and rhinestone bow out of the box Autumn brought with them, affixing it to her hair.

"Here we go Mommy!"

"She looks beautiful!" gushed Autumn. "They both, do!"

"Chrissy was pretty before, but now she's beautiful and stylish." Kirby smiled at her work and kissed the top of her head.

"Great job! I wish you lived closer to Knollwood, but if we get a house up here, you're our groomer."

"Deal!"

Ace, awake from his nap, and Chrissy, sat together near their toys, looking like they'd never been dirty in their lives. Autumn paid Kirby and gave an extra generous tip for all the information she had shared.

10

"How do you get people to open up and tell you everything? I need to learn your secret," said Ray, after Autumn shared everything she'd learned from Kirby.

"You're intimidating. Even out of uniform, it's obvious you're in law enforcement."

"Maybe I should carry Chrissy along when I do interviews." Ray smiled and petted Chrissy. In all her groomed perfection, she looked like an adorable stuffed animal.

"That could work. Like when you talk to Bobby about his dagger collection?"

"With him, I'm bringing Ace and Detective Conroy to make sure he knows we mean business." Ray dialed John Conroy, and they made plans to meet at Bobby's house.

When Ray pulled up to Bobby's white stucco cottage surrounded by scraggly bushes, he saw Detective Conroy and Officers Campos and Williams. When the suspect is likely armed, they take all precautions. Officer Williams banged on the door loud enough to wake Bobby if he was napping. She banged again, and they heard someone saying *hold your horses, I'm coming.* A disheveled Bobby Ringbottom opened the door.

"Yeah?"

"We have a warrant to search your premises," said Officer Campos, and pushed him aside as she handed it to him.

The detectives and Ace followed as Bobby stayed near the door, mouth agape, along with Officer Campos to ensure he didn't run. She guided him to the living room sofa and stood in front of him.

Ace sniffed the floor as they made their way down the hall of the tiny dwelling. The bedroom was chaotic, with an unmade bed, scuff marks on the dirty walls that were once white, and a tangle of cords surrounding the television set. A small brown, scratched cabinet with glass insets on the doors stood on a table and showed off Bobby's dagger collection.

Detective Conroy opened the cabinet door. Ace sat down in front of it.

"He smells blood," said Ray.

"Take the entire cabinet and bring it to the lab for testing," John said to Officer Williams.

She lifted the display case while the detective gave the go-ahead to Officer Campos to bring Bobby to the police station. They'd interrogate him there. Bobby's silence surprised them as they took him from his house. Not even a request for a lawyer.

Autumn called Amy to see if she wanted to come over and have lunch. She was hesitant until Autumn said that she thinks she knows why Amy was so upset the last time they got together. Either out of the need to talk to someone or because of curiosity, Amy agreed and showed up at Autumn's door at noon.

Chrissy greeted her with a wagging tail, and Amy reached down to pet her.

"She's even prettier than the last time I saw her," Amy cooed.

"I had Kirby Galloway come and groom the two of them," Autumn smiled.

Amy stopped short and hung her head. Autumn encouraged her to join her on the deck, where tuna sandwiches, pickles, iced tea, and deviled eggs awaited. Chrissy took the chair between Autumn and Amy. She patiently waited for them to share their lunch with her.

Autumn took a deviled egg and sliced a bit of egg white from the bottom. Chrissy took it gently and happily chewed the treat. She got most of the white while Autumn ate the yolk. Amy watched them as she took a bite of her tuna on toast.

"Delicious!" she said.

"I put Dijon mustard in with the mayonnaise. Gives it a kick." Autumn bit into her own sandwich.

Small talk marked most of the meal. When they finished, they cleaned up and then moved to the comfy cushioned chairs set up on the deck closer to the lake.

"I'd really like to get a place up here," said Autumn, putting Chrissy on her pet bed close by and settling into a chair.

"It's close to home and relaxing...most of the time. I'm not sure we'll stay. We've talked about selling our place. Too many terrible memories at this point with both girls gone."

"That's understandable."

"It's hard, because we have some wonderful memories, too." A tear escaped Amy's eye and ran down her face. She subtly wiped it away.

A cool breeze touched their skin, making goosebumps. Chrissy's soft hair moved with the wind, making her look like she was in a shampoo commercial.

"What can I do to help? Whatever you tell me stays between us," Autumn reassured Amy.

Amy hesitated and looked out over the lake. She took a deep breath.

"Harley and I had an affair. Loretta is the result. Barry doesn't know, or, if he does, he never said anything."

Autumn kept her eyes on the lake, as well, not wanting Amy to feel uncomfortable or judged because of this revelation. It was hard to believe that Barry was unaware, especially since Kirby Galloway knew about it.

Amy continued. "Loretta didn't know. I'm not sure if Loretta and Madison knew they were only half-sisters. At least, I didn't tell her. Neither did Harley. He gave her a job to keep an eye on her and guide her when he could. Turns out she had a mind of her own and ignored him like she ignored me."

"Does Harley have any idea who would harm Loretta and Madison?"

"I asked him. He didn't see anyone follow her into the woods or any cars in the parking area. As far as Loretta, he knew how many people disliked her. It could have been anyone she smart-mouthed, local or from out of town."

Tears streamed down Amy's face. "The police said Madison was pregnant. I didn't even know she was seeing anyone. They're doing DNA testing on the baby to see whose it is. How did I go so wrong with my daughters?" she sobbed.

Autumn handed her a box of tissues. "Not everything is in your control as a parent. I'm sure you did your best."

Chrissy stepped from her bed and pushed against Amy's leg. Amy picked her up and cuddled her. Autumn saw her breathing slow and the tears dry. Chrissy was a calming influence for those in distress. She took care of Autumn when her PTSD was at its worst and continued to do so with others. This little dog's instincts were incredible.

"I no longer have to worry about my mothering skills," she mumbled into Chrissy's hair.

"I can't imagine what you're going through, Amy. What do you need?"

"Your promise not to tell Barry."

"You have my word."

"I didn't kill Madison," said Bobby from his seat at a metal table in the interrogation room.

"Your dagger collection may tell a different story," said Ray Reed. "Whose blood is on the blades?"

He went silent.

"You seem like an intelligent guy. Give us something that points to anyone other than you," said John Conroy.

"Lawyer," insisted Bobby.

And the interview ended. An officer took him to a holding cell.

"Cathy Bailey might have information about Loretta's relationship with Bobby. She may even know something that could help us with Madison's murder," Ray suggested.

"Right," agreed John.

Ray called Autumn and let her know he and John were heading to Cathy Bailey's apartment, but he'd be home for dinner.

11

While John, Ray, and Ace were out hunting down information from Cathy Bailey, Autumn took a walk with Chrissy to the lower part of Moonlight Lake. It was a mile or so to get to Miguel's canoe rentals and the trail in that area, so Autumn brought Chrissy's stroller for when she got tired. That was a long walk on little legs. When they got closer to the lower trail, Autumn put Chrissy in the carriage and lifted the canopy to protect her from the sun.

Pushing her fur baby over the stoney terrain of the dirt trail, Chrissy bounced a bit, but expertly balanced herself on the cushion. Up ahead was Miguel's place, with a sign in bright yellow and red letters with a simple message that said, "Fun! Boat Rentals!" They came around the bend, but didn't see Miguel.

Autumn lifted Chrissy from the stroller to stretch her legs. She shook out her hair, sniffed the ground, and then trotted past the rental booth toward some bushes, dragging her pink leash along with her.

"I hope you didn't find a skunk," Autumn said. Even if the smelly animal had gone, the scent lingered and could get on the now pristine Chrissy.

She followed Chrissy and snapped up the leash before seeing what her pup had found. Her gaze found the sneakers first and followed the legs, then the torso to the face of Miguel Lopez, fixed in a look of surprise. Blood stained his white polo shirt and khaki shorts.

"This is worse than a skunk, sweetie." Chrissy looked at Autumn and wagged her tail. "Yes, you're a good girl," she said, pulling Chrissy from the dead body.

Autumn put Chrissy back in the stroller and dialed Ray.

"We'll be right there," said Ray.

Within minutes, Officers Williams and Campos pulled up to secure the scene.

"You've got quite a nose for finding bodies, little one," said Alison Williams, petting Chrissy, while Christine Campos pulled out crime scene tape and other supplies from the car.

"I enjoy your company, but I'd really rather meet you ladies and chat over lunch rather than a dead body," said Autumn, frowning.

"I can't remember this many murders so close together in my ten years on the force!" said Officer Campos.

"The detectives will find out if they're all related. Seems so, since all the victims knew Loretta," Officer Williams speculated.

Autumn silently agreed. What had Loretta gotten herself into? And how were these others involved?

Ray and John pulled up moments later with Ace in the backseat. They slammed the doors as they exited, spoke to the officers, and then looked at the body. While Detective Conroy made a call, Ray walked over to Autumn.

"It's best if you and Chrissy headed back to the cabin, or at least someplace that doesn't have a dead body in the vicinity. Can you take Ace with you? I'd feel better with him guarding you girls."

"Sure, can I get a ride? I brought the stroller, but no car."

Officer Williams overheard their conversation. "I can take you home. Hop in the front. We'll put the other two in the back with the stroller."

Autumn collapsed the stroller and put it in the backseat, along with her precious canines.

"Would you like to come in for something to drink? Are you hungry?"

"I have to get right back, but thanks. Maybe a raincheck."

Once situated back in the house, Autumn made a cup of lavender-chamomile tea with honey and put ice in it. She made Ace and Chrissy comfortable outside with cushions, water, and snacks, and then plunked down into a chair overlooking the lake. This is not how she envisioned her honeymoon. It wasn't Ray's fault. Choosing a partner who is a member of the law enforcement community was rough; personal plans often went by the wayside in favor of seeking justice for the victims of crime. They had to find the person behind the murders. This was an especially puzzling case with a very personal connection. Just because she understood didn't mean she had to like it, but she accepted who her husband was and his devotion to the job. It was one of the many things she loved about him.

She was hungry, but didn't want to cook, so she ordered food from the Log Cabin Bar, since they offered delivery.

The medical examiner determined Miguel's time of death was within three hours of the body being found. Ray thanked his lucky stars that Autumn and Chrissy hadn't gone to the boat rental location sooner, or they might be lying next to poor Miguel.

He and John thought about when they had arrested Bobby Ringbottom. It was unlikely he could have killed Miguel and then gotten home before they banged on the door. They seemed to have woken him from a deep sleep. But they couldn't account for his whereabouts when Madison and Loretta were killed. A dagger was used to kill Miguel, similar to the one that killed Loretta and Madison. And there was blood on some weapons in Bobby's collection. The lab would determine whose blood.

Someone who knew about the dagger collection could frame Ringbottom for the murders. Or Ringbottom might have a partner. They had no evidence either way. Whoever was doing this made sure they left nothing behind. They hoped the scene of Miguel's murder produced something to lead them in the right direction.

Autumn answered the door to find Danny Cole standing there holding a paper bag filled with food. Ace and Chrissy greeted him, sniffing the air and hoping for some of whatever Danny brought with him.

"Come on in, Danny," Autumn said, taking the food from his hand. "I'll be right back."

She put the food down in the kitchen and grabbed money for the order, plus a generous tip. Back in the foyer, she handed him the money and thanked him.

"How are you holding up after Loretta's service?" she asked him.

"Not great. I miss her busting my chops."

"It's funny what we miss when we lose people we love. When I lost my parents, I missed how my dad teased me about stuff and how Mom inspected my outfits before I left the house."

Danny said nothing; he just nodded. His eyes glistened, so Autumn changed the subject.

"Do you enjoy working at the bar?"

"Sure, it's okay. We'll get busier when the summer renters come to town. Right now, I can have flexible hours and take breaks to deliver food." He gave a crooked smile, one where the side of his mouth raised but contained no mirth.

Danny turned and headed toward the door with a backhanded wave.

"Take care," Autumn called after him as he pulled the door shut.

12

Amy and Barry Armstrong sat on their deck overlooking the forested property. Breathing in the scent of the woods calmed them to a degree, but nothing could make them feel right about the loss of both daughters.

"I'm thinking we should sell this house," said Amy.

"That would mean you'd have to give up on Harley," said Barry, not looking at her.

Amy kept her eyes straight ahead, not wanting Barry to see her startled expression. "There's nothing between us."

"Maybe not now," Barry said with suspicion. "But I knew something was going on. When Loretta was born, it was obvious she wasn't mine. She looked more like Harley and Madison looked more like me."

She was shocked he'd known all these years and never mentioned it.

Aching to change the subject, Amy said, "Did you know Madison was pregnant?"

"I thought she was just gaining weight. Any idea who the father was?"

"No, but they're investigating to see. It may lend itself to motive." They sat in silence.

"I love you, you know," said Barry, reaching for Amy's hand.

"I love you, too. I'm sorry that I hurt you." She squeezed his hand. "Once we find out what happened to the girls, let's go someplace where we can start over."

"Good idea."

Amy turned her head so Barry wouldn't see her tears.

Cathy Bailey answered the door to her apartment to see Detectives Reed and Conroy standing there. She wore old clothes, and the smell of bleach permeated the space.

"Can I help you?" she asked, wary of their presence.

"Mind if we come in and chat for a bit?" asked John Conroy.

She hesitated and then opened the door wider. The open concept floor plan gave the detectives a clear view of all but the bedrooms. The furniture was clear of clothing, and the kitchen had no dishes in the sink or on the counter.

"I can finally clean up," said Cathy, removing her thick rubber gloves. "Without Loretta here to make a mess, there's a chance it will stay tidy for a while. Bleach is the only thing that takes away the smell of bacon."

She sat in a side chair, leaving the couch for the detectives, but they continued to stand. Their trained eyes looked for anything suspicious.

"Mind if we see Loretta's room?" asked Ray Reed.

Cathy bit her lip. "Go ahead."

Ray nodded to John, who left the room while Ray stayed with Cathy.

"What do you hope to find?"

"We're trying to get to know the victim. Sometimes the smallest thing can lead to the killer." Ray noticed a red spot on the floor near the wall between the area rug and the molding. "Looks like you missed a spot."

Ray noticed Cathy's eyes widen. He walked over to the droplet and pulled a rubber glove, zipper bag, and a cotton swab from his pocket. He dipped the tip into the red mark, watching it absorb the color, and slid it into an evidence bag.

"When was the last time you saw Loretta?"

"Before she left for her mother's," Cathy said.

"How long did she plan to stay in Knollwood?"

Cathy gulped. "I'm not sure."

"Then why did you report her missing?"

Cathy wrung her hands and then squeezed the arms of the chair.

"How did you know what she was wearing if you hadn't seen her that day?" Ray asked, his eyes drilling into her.

"I don't remember," Cathy said, with a whine in her voice.

Ray tried a different tactic. "Aren't you afraid to be here alone?"

"Why would I be?"

"Loretta didn't drown, so what if it happened here?"

"No way that's possible!" blurted Cathy, louder than she meant to.

"Why not?"

"Be, because...," Cathy stammered, paused, "they found her in the lake!"

John Conroy emerged from the bedroom holding a bloody shirt in a gloved hand.

Cathy's mouth hung open.

"Would you mind coming with us to answer a few questions?"

"I want a lawyer," said Cathy, as the detectives escorted her out of the apartment.

Bobby Ringbottom arrived home shaken and worried about what the lab would find on the daggers. Someone could have broken in, used his daggers for God only knew what, and then put them back. The window to his bedroom had been wonky a few times, so they could have gotten in that way. The broken window lock, and the room was on the first floor, so it wouldn't be hard to steal his property and return it before he realized it was gone. That's what he would say.

He looked at the space where the display case used to be. What had he gotten himself into? This was all Madison's fault. She told him there was no need for birth control. She had it covered. He wasn't interested in being a father nor being stuck with Madison forever. Her sister was bad enough. The two of them quickly became annoying when they got together, fighting with one another and criticizing everyone around them. It got old, fast.

Bobby knew the girls' parents didn't like him; most parents didn't. Between his lack of ambition and his motorcycle, he had a terrible reputation in town. They could sense his lack of commitment and selfish nature. To him, there was nothing wrong with that. For some reason, girls loved it. He had his pick of any woman in the bars he haunted. Maybe it was the bad boy thing he'd heard about. In his early twenties, he wasn't ready to take on too much responsibility. He wanted to live for today and not worry about tomorrow.

Bobby realized the sisters competed for his attention. They didn't want him; they just didn't want the other one to have him. Like he was a great catch on unemployment for now and unsure about where he'd work once it ended. There was no long-term plan. The tiny house his parents left him before they moved to Florida was all he had. For him, that was enough. The house, his friends, and his dagger collection that was now in the police's possession.

His mind reeled at the thought of incarceration. He also thought of Madison lying on the trail stabbed to death. Would he get the blame and have free room and board for the rest of his life?

Word spread that the police had Cathy Bailey in custody. Autumn heard it from Amy, who called as soon as she found out from a neighbor of Cathy's.

"They found a shirt with blood on it!" exclaimed Amy.

"Was it Loretta's blood? Did they confirm it was her shirt?" asked Autumn.

"I don't know, but I'd be shocked if Cathy had anything to do with Loretta's murder. She put up with a lot from Loretta as a roommate. I can't think of a motive."

Autumn thought about what Cathy said at Loretta's memorial service. She sounded fed up and almost glad she had died so Cathy could get a paying roommate. She decided not to tell Amy that Loretta blackmailed Cathy for free rent.

"Let's not jump to conclusions until we have more information," counseled Autumn.

Ray walked through the door of their rental cabin to find Autumn, Chrissy, and Ace in the living room watching a movie. The sun just started going down, and it was around dinnertime.

"You hungry?" asked Autumn.

"I haven't eaten all day," he replied, sounding distracted.

"We could order a pizza."

"That sounds good. I'm going to jump in the shower."

Autumn ordered their usual half meat lovers and half veggie. By the time she fed Chrissy and Ace, Ray came out of the bedroom, wet hair combed back, and wearing cotton gym shorts with no shirt. He was in exceptionally fine condition and his abdominal and arm muscles were especially prominent. If she was a cartoon, she'd have hearts over her eyes looking at him.

"Pizza will be here in a few minutes. Looks like you had a rough day," she said, handing him an ice-cold beer.

He took a swig and smiled. "I have the best wife ever. You can always tell."

Autumn brought her own drink and settled in next to him on the couch. They talked about what the pups did all day and the lunch delivered to Autumn by Danny Cole.

"He's painfully awkward," said Autumn, feeling sorry for him.

"It could be he's uncomfortable in the presence of a beautiful woman," said Ray, kissing her lovingly on the mouth.

Chrissy took a flying leap and landed on the couch next to Autumn, then walked over her legs, ending up sprawled across both their laps.

"Not getting enough attention, eh?" Ray said, ruffling the hair on her head.

Ace came running over to get in on the action, bringing Ray a wet stuffed bear toy and dropping it at his feet. Ray picked it up and threw it across the room. Ace bounded after it and pounced on the bear, shaking it and making the paper stuffing crackle. He brought it back to Ray for a few more rounds before settling in next to him on the floor.

"I spoke to Amy today. Cathy's neighbor told her about the arrest and the bloody shirt."

"John and his team will canvas the apartment building tonight to see if anyone heard anything on the dates when Loretta was likely murdered. He knows I'm on vacation, so he'll keep me posted."

"Good." Autumn gave him a squeeze. "Just chill tonight. You need a break."

The doorbell rang. Autumn jumped up to get it, following by two barking dogs. She held them back while paying for the pizza and shut the door before they could get out.

"Shall we eat lakeside?" she asked Ray while gathering napkins.

Ray grabbed their drinks and opened the sliding door to the patio, letting Autumn go first.

In between slices, they talked about getting a mountain house.

"But maybe not here. Let's find a place where no one knows us. It's too close for comfort," said Autumn, chewing a veggie slice.

"Yeah, having a quiet place as a retreat is the idea. I'm sure your realtor friend, Maureen, will find the right place." Ray finished the last of the meat-lover's side of the pizza, put his feet up on the ottoman, and closed his eyes.

≉ 13 ≉

Cathy Bailey sat in a holding cell thinking about the police tearing apart her place, looking for more evidence. She had been careless, giving them permission to come in and search. Cathy expected Loretta's mother or sister to come and take her stuff from the apartment, but they never did. It would have been wiser to pack it up and either donate her clothes or send it to Amy Armstrong. No matter, it was too late now. They couldn't connect her to Loretta's murder as far as she could tell.

The attorney was seeing if there was enough evidence to charge her with Loretta's death. If there was, she couldn't post bail. If not, she hoped he could get her out today. She hung her head and balled her fists. Loretta continued to cause her problems. Thoughts of missed opportunities and alternative courses of action flooded her mind. A retrospective view is always clearer than an emotional in-the-moment decision.

They didn't charge Bobby Ringbottom with murder, even though they found blood on some of his daggers, so she kept hope alive. Loretta's bloody shirt could have many explanations. So could the drop of blood she hadn't cleaned. After all, Cathy wasn't stupid enough to murder Loretta and then leave the evidence in their apartment.

The entire scheme came from Bobby and Madison. And her mother, Monica. She stupidly went along with it. The plan to stop Loretta from blackmailing her by scaring Loretta into moving out started the night Bobby called her and insisted she come back to the mountains. He siphoned gas from her car while he waited for her to leave the restaurant in Knollwood. Bobby followed her until her car ran out of gas and then pulled next to her and told her to get in. It was Cathy's idea for him to make it seem like a romantic gesture.

And then things went horribly wrong.

While Ray and Ace went to see John Conroy, Autumn took Chrissy to Harley's General Store for supplies. He welcomed the fur baby into his store as long as Autumn kept her in the stroller. The thick cushion inside was like a princess seat for the little dog. She sat proudly and quietly, surveying her domain, which was anyplace she was in the moment.

They were the only shoppers in the store.

"It's always quiet before tourist season kicks off," said Harley. "Most locals don't shop during the day. They're at work."

Autumn took a leap of faith to try getting information from Harley.

"In a small community, that's understandable. I noticed word spreads fast around here. Any new grapevine news about the murders?"

"People speculate, but I don't know how accurate the grapevine is these days."

"It usually starts with a seed and works its way from there. Like with Miguel. Chrissy found him. We didn't see anyone around, but I'm surprised that no one came looking for him to rent a boat before we got there."

"Loretta proudly told me his business dropped off after she wrote a critical review."

"That's a shame. Everyone has an off day."

"Who knows, he had motive to kill my, uh, kill Loretta. There's not a lot of business to begin with and then she goes and messes with his livelihood. It's not right, and I told her so."

"What did she say?"

"She didn't care. I don't think she went back after that."

"But Miguel said she came the day she died and then he found his boat floating without her in it the next day."

"Nope. After she wrote the review, he wouldn't rent to her anymore."

Autumn wondered why Miguel lied about the boat, and if it could be the reason for his murder. Her stomach churned, thinking that he had been in the middle of a terrible situation. The lie threw off the day and time of Loretta's death, giving the killer an alibi. Who was he protecting?

Cathy's neighbors heard her and Loretta arguing so many times that it didn't seem out of the ordinary for yelling and screaming to come from the apartment. The nights Detective Conroy asked about were no different. It was quiet the week before, since Loretta wasn't in town. The noise started up again when she came back, and then no more noise after that night. The usual food smells of bacon and other meats were also absent, to everyone's relief, especially for the vegetarian down the hall. Everyone thought Loretta moved out and was grateful for the quiet, so didn't question it.

This put Loretta back home on the night the murder likely took place. That didn't mean Cathy was home with her. It could have been Bobby Ringbottom or her sister, Madison. Cathy had no alibi for that night, but showed up for work the following day. Bobby had no alibi, either. With Madison and Miguel dead, the detectives could only theorize about their involvement in Loretta's murder.

Autumn shared the information she got from Harley that Loretta never rented a boat from Miguel again after she wrote the review, so they expanded the likely dates of the murder to span a three-day period. Miguel was covering for someone, but there were no clues pointing to who it was or why.

So far, the lab confirmed that the blood on Bobby's daggers belonged to Loretta, Cathy, Bobby, and Madison. Miguel's murder occurred while the daggers were in police custody. The perpetrator wiped the handles clean, so no fingerprints. In Detective Conroy's experience, if Bobby Ringbottom had done the deed, he would most likely clean the entire weapon, not just the handle. He'd also have cuts on his hand from the knife being slippery with blood. It was looking like someone was trying to frame him.

That left Madison, since she was jealous of Loretta and Bobby. A post-mortem paternity test proved Bobby was the father. With Ringbottom's baby on the way, Madison was emotionally distraught and angry that Bobby wanted nothing to do with her or the baby.

Cathy was another potentially viable suspect, with Loretta black-mailing her and being a difficult roommate to boot. The bloody shirt and other blood spatter evidence found in the apartment only proved that Loretta had been bleeding, but it didn't prove that the stabbing occurred in the apartment or who was responsible. As such, they released Cathy.

He had to find the crime scene from Loretta's murder, and then the others would fall into place.

Ray hung up and turned to Autumn.

"Brainstorming with John Conroy is stimulating, but didn't get us farther along the path to finding a killer."

"You're missing both the who and the where," said Autumn, as she made them a picnic lunch of fluffernutter sandwiches, Caesar salad, and lemonade, along with kibble, water, and snacks for the pups. She hoped that salad would complement the sweetness of the peanut butter and marshmallow crème sandwich. Being honest with herself, there weren't too many foods that go with a fluffernutter, but it made her feel better to add something green to the mix.

"Right. Where did you want to picnic?"

"The map shows a trail near the lake that leads to a picnic area. It looks like a pleasant walk to get there, and there are picnic tables, so we don't have to sit on the ground. I'll bring a blanket for Chrissy and Ace."

She loaded everything into a backpack, affixed harnesses and leashes to Chrissy and Ace, and off they went down the road toward the trailhead, holding hands. The woods looked denser than on other trails they'd been down. The trees made a tunnel, partially blocking the sun. It seemed they were walking into a shadowy world that was completely private. From what they could tell, this park served the residents of this community rather than being public like the others they had gone down.

"It's beautiful back here. I feel like we walked through a portal to another world," said Autumn.

"It certainly feels otherworldly," Ray agreed. "It's the densest and greenest trail we've been on."

Ace and Chrissy padded down the short trail, eager to explore the unfamiliar scents of the area and actively sniffing for animals. They marked where they wanted to establish their territory.

The picnic tables were up ahead. Ace stuck his long nose into some shrubs and sat down, unwilling to move until Ray had a look. Chrissy checked it out with mild interest before walking over to Autumn to be picked up. Ray separated the branches and saw smears of red on the leaves. He reached back to pet Ace.

They continued down the path toward the empty tables and saw faded red smears on the closest one. Ace sat next to that table while Autumn carried Chrissy to the far part of the picnic area. Ray dialed John Conroy.

Officers Campos and Williams were first on the scene.

"You guys really have a nose for finding crime scenes," said Alison Williams, as she cordoned off the area.

"Ace found this one," said Ray proudly. "We just wanted a peaceful place to eat lunch."

Christine Campos worked around the shrub on the trail and greeted Detective Conroy when he arrived.

"Looks like we may have found the crime scene. It fits. Close to the lake. A secluded area. I could see a murder happening here at night," John said to Ray.

"There are drag marks in the grass and on the edge of the trail. It would be easy to drag a victim into the lake," added Officer Campos.

"We'll know more once we confirm the blood is Loretta's. I'll keep you posted. You folks get back to your lunch," said John.

"Is there another way back to our cabin? I don't want to disturb the area," Ray asked.

John walked them to an alternate trail leading out of the picnic area. He stopped and looked around. "I just realized this is a shortcut to Cathy Bailey's apartment building."

"Meaning that the killer could have murdered Loretta in the picnic area and dragged her to the lake, and then backtracked and made it to the apartment unseen," said Autumn. She shivered, thinking about the nefarious acts that go on in the world masked by darkness and thick woods.

"Or," Ray added, "the murder started in the apartment and ended here. Maybe Loretta tried to get away, and the killer finished the job here. That would explain the blood droplet I found at the apartment."

John nodded.

They ate their picnic lunch in silence down on the dock. The text chime on Autumn's phone showed an alert from Amy Armstrong with details for Madison's memorial service.

"Madison's service is being held at the Campbell's Funeral Home in Stroudsburg. It's happening next week."

"The medical examiner must have released the body."

"Next week is our last week up here. I hope we find the killer soon."

Ray looked at her. "Me, too."

A splashing sound in the lake made Chrissy bark and Ace stand at attention. The tip of a canoe came around a shrub that blocked visibility. As the boat came into view, Danny Cole waved as Ace growled and Chrissy continued to bark.

"Hey, Danny," called Autumn. "You off today?"

"I figured I'd get in a little rowing time before the bar and the lake get too busy in the next few weeks."

"Glad you can take some time to relax," she responded.

The dogs continued to bark, so Danny said farewell and paddled off toward the middle of the lake. As soon as his back was to their dock and the boat was twenty yards away, Ace and Chrissy stopped barking.

"Way to protect us, kids!" said Ray, petting them both at the same time.

"He's harmless," Autumn assured him. "Just awkward."

"Until we know who's committing these crimes, I want you to stay alert, especially when I'm not here. Ace stays with you until this investigation is over."

"Yes, dear," she replied lovingly and gave him a grateful kiss. She liked Ray's protective nature.

Cathy lay on her couch watching television, jumping at every little sound. Clattering in the apartment next door. Footsteps in the hallway coming toward her door. Ray's words, asking if she was afraid to stay in the apartment alone, turned over in her head. After all, Madison and Miguel were dead, and Loretta was just as connected to her, if not more.

She wished she had a friend she could invite over, but she didn't trust anyone, especially Bobby Ringbottom. Her mother was out of the question. She usually increased Cathy's anxiety rather than calmed it. Monica had contributed to the plan and pushed her to make it happen, so there was no escape or distraction from interacting with her mother. Applications to rent Loretta's room were non-existent, so she couldn't busy herself with that task. Cathy thought about going out to the Tall Tree Inn to get some dinner. She hadn't been there since Loretta died. When she was working, Loretta used to slip extra food on Cathy's plate or give her a dessert and not charge her for it. It was one of the few times Loretta gave her something rather than taking.

It was strange going into the place, knowing Loretta wasn't there. Lily came up to her and gave her a hug.

"How are you doing? Are you okay?" asked Lily.

"As well as expected, I guess."

"Are you here with anyone?"

"Just me." Cathy never felt so lonely.

"I'll take care of you." Lily patted Cathy on the shoulder. "Do you want to sit inside or outside?"

"On the porch is good."

Lily led her outside and put her at a table overlooking the rushing creek. The sound soothed Cathy's frazzled nerves somewhat, but her regrets and fears played endlessly in her mind. She ordered a Rueben, and Lily brought her a side of cheese fries on the house. Being out of the apartment helped her body relax. Not being in a place that held Loretta's energy and memories of their last violent argument gave her a respite. She finished eating, paid the check minus the cheese fries, and left.

Lily watched her go and picked up the phone.

"She just left."

The calm from the meal and sounds of the rushing creek were temporary. Cathy walked to her car, jumping at every sound. Night had fallen over the forest surrounding the restaurant, so Cathy attributed every sound to the killer, including the sounds of woodland creatures. She couldn't shake the sense of eyes on her as she got into her car. Cathy slammed the door closed and hit the locks.

The five-minute drive home encapsulated her in safety, but when she pulled into her apartment building's parking lot, she hesitated to get out of the car. Maybe she should go stay at her mother's house, or even a motel, but nixed both ideas. Monica would chastise her for being weak, which she wasn't in the mood for, and she didn't like the idea of sleeping on a motel bed that so many others stayed in.

She sat with the engine off and the doors locked, looking around the tree line that surrounded the old converted mansion. It was getting hot in the car with the windows up, so she turned the key and rolled down the windows a couple of inches. Air flowed in, giving her some relief. She listened for movement. Every scary movie she'd ever seen where the killer hid waiting for the victim came into her mind.

There were some lights on in the windows. If she screamed, would anyone hear her? The fifty feet between Cathy's car and the side entrance seemed miles away, but she couldn't sit in the car all night. She rolled up the windows, gave one more look around the area, and opened the car door, listening for anything suspicious before fully getting out of her car.

"You're being ridiculous," she scolded herself.

She shut the door and hit the lock button on the key fob. As she came around the side of the car, a hand pulled back her head, exposing her neck. The lights in the building faded as her life slipped away.

15

The phone call dashed their plans to sleep in. Ray hung up and closed his eyes as he shared the news.

"They found Cathy Bailey dead this morning. According to the medical examiner, it happened sometime last night."

"Oh, no!" said Autumn.

Chrissy pawed at her mommy for a belly rub. Ace lay next to Ray with his front leg across Ray's stomach.

"It's got to be Bobby Ringbottom," said Autumn.

"We can't jump to conclusions. I know you want the murders to stop and for Loretta and Madison to get justice so Amy has closure," Ray said, rubbing Autumn's back. He sighed. "I have to meet John at the scene."

Autumn watched him head to the bathroom, rubbing the pups, who were blissfully lounging in bed. She wished she could be as oblivious to what was going on as they were.

Ray kissed Autumn goodbye and scratched the heads of the pups. "I'll try to get back soon. Keep your phone on and Ace nearby."

Chrissy jumped off the bed and chased after Ray, doing two laps of zoomies in the living room while Ace barked at her playfully.

"Okay, guys. I'll be home soon." Ray planted a kiss on each of them and left.

"What have we got, John?" asked Ray, treading carefully around the crime scene.

He shook his head. "Cathy Bailey, killed in front of her own home last night."

"Was a weapon used?"

"A knife. The medical examiner said she had food in her stomach and had just come from dinner."

"Good thing there are only a few restaurants around here."

"She went to the Tall Tree Inn. Lily Harding served her dinner around seven-forty-five. Cathy left around nine o'clock."

"Tall Tree Inn isn't far from here, so it puts the time of death no later than 9:30 pm."

"Around there. We checked, and it doesn't look like she made any stops on the way home."

Ray's voice expressed disappointment as he stated, "I really thought Cathy was a viable suspect."

"We still have Bobby Ringbottom."

"But we have his dagger collection."

"Wouldn't stop him from using a regular knife to do the deed, which is what the medical examiner thinks it was."

"Call me when that's confirmed."

John Conroy nodded. "Will do."

Chrissy sniffed the base of the bushes while Autumn and Ace waited. Since Ray had the SUV, they walked around the neighborhood. Autumn didn't want to revisit the path and picnic area where they found blood.

A woman walked toward them. She looked vaguely familiar. Ace growled, and Autumn told him to be nice and waved at the woman.

"I've seen you around," she said.

"Yes. We're renting the cabin over there." Autumn pointed.

"You found Loretta."

"That's right."

"You're friends with Amy Armstrong."

Autumn frowned. "What of it?"

Ace growled again, but Autumn didn't correct him. She remembered the woman pacing on the bluff at Loretta's memorial service.

"She stole Harley from me!" the woman yelled.

Ace bared his teeth. Chrissy shook and hid behind Autumn's leg.

"You're upsetting the dogs."

"I don't care. If you're her friend, then I'm your enemy!"

"Ace is a trained police dog!"

As the woman charged at Autumn, Ace launched, taking her to the ground and standing on her chest. The woman continued screaming and cursing as Ray pulled into the driveway, saw the commotion, and came running.

"Ace, come!"

Ace bared his teeth and gave the woman one last stare before he obeyed.

"She came at me. Ace protected me."

"Good boy," said Ray. He grabbed the woman's arm and lifted her to her feet. "Are you looking to get arrested? What's your name?"

The woman scowled. "Monica Bailey."

"Cathy's mother?" asked Autumn.

"Yes! Somebody killed my baby! It's Amy's fault!"

She stood up and brushed herself off. "Harley Waters was her father. Amy stole him from me."

"I'm so sorry for your loss. It's understandable you're upset about Cathy, but why the anger at Amy? After all these years, what difference could it make?" asked Autumn.

"Loretta found out Harley was her father and was blackmailing him for money, threatening to tell Barry Armstrong. Harley told me. She was taking money from my Cathy, too. It's all Amy's fault for getting pregnant with Loretta."

"Did Cathy know Harley was her father?" asked Ray.

"No. I gave her my surname to protect her from any scandal and said her father was a Marine who died in Afghanistan. She knew Loretta was blackmailing Harley, but not why."

"Cathy didn't know Loretta was her half-sister and vice versa?"

"No."

Roy made a call and then said, "We need you to go down to the station, Ms. Bailey."

A police car pulled up, and Alison Williams jumped out, cuffed Monica Bailey, and put her into the backseat.

"Thanks, Alison."

"My pleasure," she said with a smile.

"I'll be right behind you. I'll let John know we're on our way."

Ace stood next to Autumn. She held Chrissy in her arms. Ray kissed her goodbye and petted the pups, who had Autumn's safety well in hand.

16

At the station, Monica Bailey sat across from Detective John Conroy with her arms crossed and wearing a scowl. Lieutenant Ray Reed watched from an observation room since his wife was involved in the attack. It was best for him to maintain an objective role in the interrogation.

"What made you attack Autumn?" asked John.

"I had to stand up for my daughter!" she yelled, her body stretching across the table.

"Tell me more about that," John said calmly, his expression neutral.

"She's dead, and it's Loretta's fault. Amy made Loretta with Harley, who was mine. She stole him from me when I was pregnant with Cathy. Autumn is friends with Amy. Anyone associated with Amy is my enemy!"

"When did you make this decision?"

She hesitated. "When I got the news that someone murdered Cathy."

"What stopped you from going after Amy when she got pregnant?"

"Harley! He talked me out of it. If the word got out, he could lose business. All the years he'd worked hard to build it would have been for nothing."

"And what of the consequences to Amy?"

"Harley told me he didn't love her. He loved me. Plus, if her husband found out, she'd wind up alone and wanting Harley even more."

John watched her face. Sweat beaded her upper lip and her chest turned red. She was holding back information.

"When did your relationship with Harley end?"

Monica balled her fists and slammed them against the table.

"When I realized he was still seeing Amy. I couldn't be in a three-way relationship. He voluntarily gave me support money until Cathy was 18 years old to avoid court." Monica growled the words and spat as though they were toxic.

"But Amy is still with her husband," John pointed out.

Ray watched, mesmerized by Monica's delusions about the situation, and wondered if she played a role in the recent deaths.

Monica stared at John Conroy, perplexed by the question. Ray watched it dawn on her that Harley lied about why they couldn't be together.

"No matter, Loretta had to go," Monica said, not looking at the detective.

"How did you make sure of that?"

"That idiot, Bobby Ringbottom. He's just like Harley, being with two women at once and getting Madison pregnant."

"What did he do?"

"He's the only one who listened to me about Loretta poisoning the group. She was born of evil and betrayed everyone around her, just like her mother."

Years of anger reddened Monica's face. She bared her teeth.

"Did you convince Bobby to kill Loretta?"

She stopped, gave a wicked grin, and said, "I want an attorney."

An officer escorted Monica Bailey to a cell, as Ray and John debriefed about the interview.

"I called a psychiatrist to evaluate Monica. Something is off with her," said John.

"I agree. But I've seen glimmers of truth within the strangest stories. We need to get Ringbottom back here to question him about his relationship with Monica Bailey," said Ray.

John instructed two officers to pick him up.

Autumn sat outside the cabin, trying to relax. Chrissy and Ace sat next to her chair like protective foo dogs, guardian lions from Chinese culture. The altercation with Monica Bailey wound her up, making a restorative nap out of the question. Instead, she had called Amy Armstrong to warn her of the vendetta.

Monica's long-held grudge didn't surprise Amy, but Monica's attack on Autumn shocked her.

"Good thing Ace was there," said Amy. "This situation keeps coming back to bite me. One indiscretion, and the ripples of it have lasted over two decades. I finally talked to Barry about it."

"Did he know about Harley?" Autumn asked gently.

"Yes. He's known all this time. We're starting over, selling the house up here, and focusing on healing our marriage. Besides, with the girls murdered up here, the area is depressing."

"That's understandable. Better to be in Knollwood for now."

"We already called Maureen to put the house on the market." Amy sighed. "I've always loved this place, but there are too many dreadful memories now. It's better to be away from Harley, too, for Barry's sake."

"Did you know that Cathy Bailey was Harley's daughter?"

Silence at the other end of the phone. Autumn preferred face-to-face conversations to have body language cues coupled with vocal fluctuations. Ray shared how to observe changes during an interview and use them to gain useful information. She heard a deep sigh.

"Yes." Amy's depression was palpable.

"Did Cathy and Loretta know they were half-sisters?"

A groan came through the line.

"They found out through one of those DNA websites. That's when they moved in together and Loretta began torturing Cathy. Blackmailing her and Harley."

Monica told Autumn they didn't know about one another. That, plus the blackmail-for-free-rent scheme, were excellent motives for Cathy to murder Loretta. But with Cathy dead, she hoped Ray would come up with a way to uncover her involvement. With the many people Loretta Armstrong alienated, the number of suspects could include any of them. They'd all known one another long enough to have built-up resentments that turned into the desire for revenge.

Bobby Ringbottom was back at the police station, sitting on an uncomfortable metal chair in the interrogation room. Having two detectives stare at him made him squirm. Sweat ran down his back despite the low temperature in the room.

"The lab results are in," said John Conroy.

Bobby didn't say a word.

"There was blood from Loretta and Madison on various daggers," John continued.

Bobby pressed his lips together.

"What do you have to say for yourself?"

He looked at Detective Conroy and over to the steel gaze of Lieutenant Ray Reed.

"I don't know what to say, other than someone's trying to frame me."

"What makes you think that?" asked Ray.

"I'm not stupid enough to kill someone and not clean the weapon afterward. Besides, it's easy to break into my house. Go check the lock on the bedroom window."

Detective Conroy made a note to do that.

"Where were you the afternoon Madison was killed?" Ray asked.

"I heard about it the next day. The day before, I was with my buddy, Al, over at his place in Mt. Pocono playing video games."

Lieutenant Reed pushed a pad and pen toward Boddy. "Write his name and contact information, please."

Bobby did so.

"And how about last night, around 9:30 pm?" asked John Conroy.

"Watching TV at my house."

"Can anyone verify that?"

"I was alone, if that's what you mean."

"What's your relationship with Monica Bailey?"

Bobby's mouth dropped open. "I don't have one."

"She told us she convinced you that Loretta was toxic and to do away with her."

"She's just crazy and jealous."

"How would you know that if you had no relationship with her?"

"Cathy told me."

"So, you and Cathy were friends?"

"Couldn't avoid her since she lived with Loretta."

"Did you know Loretta was blackmailing Cathy? Did Cathy ask for your help to make her stop?"

Bobby clasped his hands together so that his knuckles turned white.

"How did Loretta get back up here from Knollwood?"

Ringbottom crossed his arms.

"I want a lawyer."

"OK, we'll check out the window."

John Conroy nodded. An officer came into the room, cuffed Bobby, and escorted him to a cell.

"They knew, Ray. They knew about being half-sisters!"

He had just walked in the door and his head was still in Bobby Ringbottom's interrogation. Ray looked at Autumn to focus on what she was talking about.

"Who?"

"Loretta Armstrong and Cathy Bailey. Harley fathered both of them. Couldn't that be a motive?"

"For what?"

"Maybe Cathy killed Loretta. Or maybe Monica killed Loretta and Madison; Loretta for blackmailing her daughter and Madison for revenge against Amy."

"So, who killed Cathy? And why?"

"Maybe Bobby Ringbottom?"

"He was out and about at the time of her murder. But did he know they were half-sisters? And if he did, would he care? What's his motive for killing Cathy?"

Autumn crossed her arms and tapped her lip, her pose for being stumped.

"I don't know. Let's ponder it over dinner. Log Cabin Restaurant?"

"Sure."

The hostess knew them from the last time they were there. She remembered Chrissy and Ace and how well-behaved they were. She seated them at a lake view table.

"Madison's funeral is tomorrow. It's at a funeral home, so we'll have to leave the pups at home," said Autumn, looking over the menu.

"It will be interesting to see who shows up for the service."

The server came to their table with drinks and took their order, including the meatloaf special for the pups that had no garlic, onion, or other ingredients harmful to dogs.

The number of people at Madison's funeral was less than at Loretta's. Including Autumn and Ray, there were ten people dressed in dark clothing who made it past the closed casket to speak to Amy and Barry Armstrong in hushed, concerned tones. The occasion was more somber than Loretta's beach service. Amy didn't get behind the podium to speak about her daughter. A minister conducted a brief service. None of the mourners came up to speak. The entire occasion concluded in an hour.

Autumn approached Amy and said, "Whatever you need, I'll be there," knowing there was really nothing to be done that would make a difference to a grieving mother. Especially one who had lost not one, but two offspring.

As they walked back to the car, Autumn said, "My heart breaks for Amy."

Ray put his arm around her, pulling her toward him. He kissed the top of her head and helped her into the SUV.

"Tell me you're close to finding out who did this."

"We're doing our best," he said, squeezing her hand. "I'll take you home, and then I'm meeting up with John Conroy."

Autumn nodded.

At the police station, Ray found out that Bobby was ready to talk after being encouraged by his lawyer, who sat next to him during the interview.

Ray and John were opposite him at the table, maintaining an open posture to signal they will consider what he had to say.

"This whole thing is freaking me out," Bobby began. "All these people being killed. I have nothing to do with it."

"Let's back up and start from the night Loretta had dinner with friends," Ray suggested in a friendly tone, as though they were buddies and Bobby was relaying a funny story.

Bobby looked at his attorney and got a nod. He gulped.

"Loretta went to stay at her mom's after we had a big fight."

"What were you fighting about?" asked John.

"Her sister, Madison. She hated Madison for flirting with me and suspected we sleeping together."

"Were you?" asked Ray, trying not to sound accusatory.

Bobby looked down at his clenched hands.

"Yes. Madison got pregnant and hounded me to break up with Loretta. So, we made a plan, along with Cathy Bailey, to bring her back up here and tell her how things were going to be."

"Meaning...?" John said, trying to clarify what happened.

"That she and I would break up and she'd stop blackmailing Cathy." Bobby sighed. "I called her from outside the restaurant while she was out with friends and made it sound like I wanted to make up. She didn't buy it and had no plans to come back for a few days. We didn't want to wait that long."

Ray thought how impulsive this group of young people was. If they had waited until Loretta came back on her own, things may be different. Their perspectives might have changed. Maybe Loretta would still be alive. Maybe Madison and Cathy would be, too.

Bobby continued. "After she hung up on me, I siphoned gas from her car and left enough that she'd run out a little way down the road. I was surprised she started heading north. Maybe she did want to talk to me after all. We followed her. Then Cathy and I grabbed her, put her in the backseat of my car, and drove to their apartment. She was yelling and kicking the seat the whole way, saying she would kill us when we got home." He took a gulp of water.

"When we got there, Madison was waiting. She and Loretta started screaming at each other. Cathy tried separating the two. Madison had one of my daggers and stabbed Loretta in the arm."

"How did she happen to have your dagger?" Ray asked.

Bobby looked down. "The girls told me they took daggers from my collection. Just to scare Loretta, not to hurt her. Somehow, Loretta got the dagger away from her and used it on Madison."

That explained one of the stab wounds on Madison's corpse. But not all of them, John thought.

"Go on," John encouraged him.

"Cathy pulled a dagger from her purse and stabbed Loretta in the chest. Her mother, Monica, egged her on every chance she got."

Bobby was sweating. His hands were shaking.

"I tried taking the daggers away from them and cut myself. This wasn't how it was supposed to go down."

"Was Monica there?" asked John Conroy.

"No."

"What happened next?" asked Ray.

"Madison took the knife away from Loretta and went nuts. I couldn't get her to stop. When Loretta stopped moving, that's when she backed off." He sighed. "We dragged her through the park to get to the lake and threw her in. Then Cathy reported her missing."

"What did Miguel have to do with the murder?" Ray wanted all the information he could get now that Bobby was talking.

"Nothing. We asked him to lie to throw off the police and paid him a hundred bucks to help us."

It was John's turn. "Did you kill Cathy and Madison?"

"Hell, no! That's why I decided to talk to you guys. Somebody else killed them. I'm afraid I'm next!"

Bobby put his head in his hands and sobbed.

≈ 18 ≈

Autumn walked into the Tall Tree Inn with Ace and Chrissy in tow. Lily recognized her because of the pups and seated them on the patio and handed Autumn a menu.

"Dining alone today?"

"Of course not," Autumn answered, waving her hand toward her furry dining companions.

"Right," Lily said, and smiled.

Autumn laid their blanket down and filled bowls of water.

"Can I get them anything?"

"No, that's okay. I brought their food."

Autumn took two more bowls and filled them with kibble and topped them off with ground beef crumbles.

Lily gave her a moment to look at the menu and told her the specials. Autumn ordered the salmon special and a side salad.

"Be right up," Lily said and walked away. Autumn's attention was on the roaring creek below the patio and didn't notice that Chrissy followed Lily out of the room.

Chrissy sniffed the floor and followed the scent to where Lily sat on the phone at the hostess station.

"Yes, she's here now. Her cop husband isn't here. Just the dogs. Uh, huh, uh, huh. I don't know when they're leaving, but I'll call you when they do." She hung up and spotted Chrissy looking up at her and wagging her tail. "What are you doing, little one? You have to go back to your spot outside." She picked up the fluff ball and carried her to Autumn.

"I'm so sorry! I didn't realize she had gone inside the restaurant," said Autumn.

She took Chrissy from Lily and snuggled her close. "You need to stay with Mommy and Ace, little girl."

Chrissy licked her cheek. Lily walked away. Autumn put her forehead to Chrissy's and saw Lily on the phone. She heard her voice and read her lips, shocked at what she saw Lily saying to an unknown person at the other end of the line. Autumn had no desire to encounter whoever Lily planned to tip off when she left the restaurant, so she called Ray. It went to voicemail, and she left a message for him to meet her at the Tall Tree Inn. She would sit here until he arrived, even if she had to order everything on the menu.

The *urgent* notation included in Autumn's message alarmed Ray. With all the craziness going on, he was uncomfortable anytime she went out by herself, even with Ace covering her. After listening to the message, he knew Lily hadn't spoken to Bobby or Monica, since they had them in custody. The other conspirators that they knew of were dead. Who had she spoken to about tipping them off when Autumn left the restaurant? He thanked their lucky stars for Chrissy's special talent. Without it, this may have never come to light.

With Bobby safely back in his cell, Ray headed over to the Tall Trees Inn. Lily saw him and pulled back, startled.

"Hi, Lily," he said, and waved, as though he didn't suspect a thing.

"H, h, hi," Lily stammered. "Autumn is on the patio with the pups."

"Thanks."

When Autumn saw him, she leaped from her chair and hugged him tight. The pups came running over, too. Ray loved the way his little family appreciated him.

"I'm so glad to see you!" said Autumn, giving him one more squeeze. "How did you get here? Are you hungry?"

"John Conroy gave me a loaner car saying it was official business when I told him about your message. Yeah, I could eat. Besides, hanging out here might give us more information about Lily's shenanigans."

He saw Lily peek around the corner and approach them with a menu.

"I know what I want. The Cuban sandwich. It was so good last time. And a Coke."

"Coming right up." She tried sounding chipper, but Ray homed in on the nervous undertone in her voice.

"You, okay?" Ray whispered.

"Much better now that you're here." Autumn reached for his hand. "I don't understand what's going on, but thinking about the night of Cathy Bailey's murder, she was here first. Could Lily have made a call that night, too?"

"It's possible. Seems like too much of a coincidence."

Autumn nodded as she sipped ice tea.

Chrissy pawed at Ray's leg. He picked her up and told her what a good girl she was for letting them know about Lily.

"Maybe you can trace the number Lily dialed."

"Did you see if she was on a cell phone or the restaurant landline?"

"Chrissy's vision wasn't that specific."

"Well, we know she didn't call Bobby. We were interrogating him when you sent me the message."

"Getting a confession, I hope."

"Yes, and no. He distanced himself from the crime and blamed it on Cathy Bailey and Madison Armstrong, with Monica Bailey as one of the masterminds. Too bad we can't do any follow-up questioning. I'm not sure how much of what he said is true, but some of what he said supports the evidence we found in the apartment and the picnic area. And I believe him when he said he's scared."

"Of what?"

"The person who killed Cathy, Madison, and Miguel. He's afraid he's next."

Lily came to the table with Ray's order and put the plate and drink in front of him with a slightly trembling hand. It smelled heavenly and made him realize how hungry he was.

"Will there be anything else right now?" Lily asked.

"Nope, we're all set," said Ray with a smile.

She wasn't as chatty as she was when they first met. When she walked away, Autumn noticed her unsteady gait.

"Lily has seemed nervous since I walked in," Ray said, and then took a healthy bite of his sandwich.

"I'll visit the restroom," said Autumn with a smirk.

She left the patio and entered the main restaurant area through the sliding glass doors, looking for Lily under the guise of finding the ladies' room. Autumn saw Lily huddled in the corner on her cell phone and padded over to her as quietly as she could.

"He's here now. You have to call it off," Lily growled, urgency in her voice. "No. The dogs are here, too. Don't take the chance!"

Autumn heard her clearly despite whispering in the device. Lily hung up and turned to see Autumn standing there. She let out a moan as her cheeks reddened and her eyes teared up.

Autumn smiled. "Can you tell me where the restroom is?"

Lily pointed a shaking finger.

"Thanks."

Confronting her right then would be a mistake, but now she knew Lily had made the call on a cell phone. She'd leave it to Ray to find out who was at the other end.

Ray followed Autumn back to the house. Ace and Chrissy rode in her vehicle, just in case. He trusted Ace to keep her safe if they somehow got separated. Vigilant to movement or cars following them, Ray's training would alert him to anything suspicious. Catching the person who'd been creating a deadly atmosphere in the formerly peaceful community was a priority, but so was getting Autumn and the furry kids safely inside.

When they pulled up, John Conroy sat in his unmarked black cruiser.

"Hey, John," said Ray, shaking his hand.

John smiled and looked at Autumn. "Thanks to your sleuthing, we know who Lily's been talking to."

"Who?"

"It's more like 'where,' since it went to a burner phone. No name associated with it. They likely paid cash."

"Was the 'where' helpful?"

"It pinged in this neighborhood. With Lily ready to tell this unknown person when you left the restaurant, that worries me. Just because she told them not to pursue whatever the plan was, doesn't mean they won't try."

A patrol car pulled up across the street, and Officers Williams and Campos got out.

"I see the gang's all here," said Christine Campos.

"After what I heard about Ace's protective abilities, I'm surprised anyone would try to come near your place," said Alison Williams.

Autumn went over and hugged the women.

"They'll be stationed out front here and periodically check the lakeside. That way you can get some rest," said John.

"Much appreciated. Maybe I can take a shift, too," offered Ray.

"Uh, this is our regular shift this week, so we're good," assured Officer Campos.

"Besides, you're supposed to be on vacation. A honeymoon, I believe?" Officer Williams smiled.

Autumn punch Ray's arm, playfully. "Yeah, that's right."

"Okay, okay," said Ray.

"Sleep tight," said Detective Conroy before getting in his car and driving off.

"Can I get you anything to eat or drink?" said Autumn.

"No, thanks. We're good. Go relax," said Officer Williams.

But Autumn was on edge and, despite Ray's best romantic efforts, couldn't stop thinking about a murderer lurking in the dark around their house. Even with Ace sitting in front of the window, eyes watching for anything that moved, her nerves told her not to let her guard down. They watched a movie, tried to sleep, got up and drank water. Autumn laid back down, and stared at the ceiling. Now she knew how Ace felt most of the time, hypervigilant and waiting to alert his family to any danger.

She finally dozed off at some point. When she opened her eyes, the sun streamed through the arched window in the bedroom, peeking over the top of the drapes. She was alone. No Ray. No pups. She heard voices in the kitchen. Throwing on a sweatshirt and shorts, she went out to see Ray, Christine, and Alison having coffee. Ace and Chrissy were enjoying some kibble mixed with scrambled eggs. Ray kissed Autumn and poured her a cup of coffee. She hopped onto a stool, joining them at the kitchen island.

"All quiet last night, I take it," said Autumn, and sipped her coffee. Ray made excellent coffee.

"There was a raccoon, a couple of deer, and an owl," said Alison, with a chuckle.

"Thank goodness for that," Autumn replied.

"You still never know. The suspect could just hide out or delay their plans because of the police presence," said Ray. Alison and Christine nodded in agreement.

Ray's phone rang. John Conroy was at the other end, letting him know they released Monica after her psych evaluation yesterday. Unless Autumn pressed assault charges, they couldn't hold her.

"She won't do that. Besides, I'm hopeful Ace scared her enough to back off," said Ray. "But if she was out yesterday, there's a chance she's the one Lily called."

"We have the number Lily called and dialed it several times. There was no answer. My guess is whoever it belongs to tossed it."

"I'll stay watchful at this end. Alison and Christine are heading out. Thanks for the protection, John."

"Right. Don't let your guard down."

With everything that happened, Ray and Autumn spent the day at home and took the pups for a canoe ride. With the house locked up, everyone donned their life jackets and launched from the dock behind the house. Autumn looked back at the house, picturing Ray with a tray of French toast and the high hopes they had for a peaceful honeymoon. She thought a second attempt at a vacation was called for.

As they paddled, the boats were close enough to talk at normal volume. Sound carried across the water, so they were careful about what they were saying.

"Ray, this trip hasn't been what we planned. After this is over, let's look at other places we could go with Chrissy and Ace."

"Agreed. Let's try Rehoboth Beach in Delaware. We could rent a place on the ocean."

"Sounds heavenly. I heard the shopping is great, too. We just have to confirm that it's dog friendly."

"Of course."

They lost themselves in the gentle sounds of their oars moving the water. Another canoe moved slowly up ahead. Ace got up from his prone position and watched. It turned and came toward them. Ace growled. Ray was on alert. Autumn hung back. And then the paddler waved. It was Danny Cole. They waved back, but Ace continued to growl, and Ray didn't stop him. Chrissy stood up to see what was going on, and put her paws on the side of the canoe.

As he came closer, Autumn said, "Hey, Danny. Got the day off?"

"Just the morning. I have to go in this afternoon. So, if you need food delivered, I'll be on the job in time for dinner." He gave them a toothy grin.

Autumn gave a wan smile, feeling sorry for him. His energy screamed how ill at ease he was, and she hoped he'd become more confident with more life experience.

"You seem to prefer this lake. It's the second time we've run into you," said Ray.

"That's because there's a public access boat launch where I can bring my canoe and put it in without living on the lake or paying a fee to rent a boat."

"Makes sense," said Autumn.

Danny looked at his watch. "Gotta go. See ya!" Danny said and paddled away toward the lower part of the lake where Miguel's business used to be. His back muscles bulged with each stroke of the oar.

"Bye!" said Autumn.

"You don't see many young folks wearing watches these days, especially around water," Ray commented. "They usually look at their phone for the time."

"Some do. I read that forty-five percent of people wear watches, and they're making a comeback among the younger crowd. It could be a gift and waterproof. Besides, I don't always have my cell phone with me."

"True," said Ray, skeptically.

"Why?"

"It seems I've seen that watch before, but I can't remember where."

"I'm sure it will come to you. The sun is strong today, and I'm feeling a little crispy. Let's head back and get under the umbrella."

"Race you!"

19

Monica Bailey tore through her house, smashing pictures of Cathy and Harley. How dare they make her get judged by a psychiatrist looking for her deepest secrets? What do they know about her life and why she went after Autumn Reed? How dare she be friends with Amy Armstrong? She was sick of people assuming things about her and angry that her life ended up like this, without a man and without her daughter.

Bobby was supposed to get rid of Loretta, not Cathy. Loretta was the source of her pain. And losing her would hurt Amy Armstrong. But then she still had her husband and a daughter, so that had to be taken from her, as well. She was tired of Amy coming to the mountains and flaunting her good fortune, smiling at everyone, and having no regrets. When Harley hired Loretta at the store, Monica blew a gasket, knowing that her father was taking an interest in her, but not in his daughter Cathy.

Having Cathy live with Loretta was supposed to get her out of their lives, but her daughter wasn't supposed to be involved in the murder. She blamed Bobby for being dumb as a rock and not listening to instructions. His wandering eye complicated things, between him being with Loretta, and then getting her sister, Madison, pregnant, and finally wanting Lily Harding. He didn't know which end was up, although she knew which end his brain lived in.

With Lily helping her track Autumn Reed's whereabouts, she could take one more swing at her, but not if the dogs were there. That big German Shepherd Dog scared the daylights out of her, and so did her very large, fit cop husband. She could tell he was protective of his wife. Monica thought she should be so lucky as to have a solid relationship with a good man. But she never had been. Even in high school, her boyfriends only wanted quick physical interactions from her. There was no long-term commitment, not even from other females, so when she became pregnant with Harley's child, she figured he'd have to commit to her for the long haul. But he hadn't. In fact, he never married. Monica decided it was because he pined for Amy.

Now she had a decision to make: go after Bobby, Amy, or Autumn. Maybe all three deserved punishments for the part they played in destroying her life and Cathy's life. All this resentment made her hungry, so she headed over to Tall Trees Restaurant, hoping Lily was working.

Lily was glad when Autumn, her husband, and the dogs were gone. She wondered why they hadn't confronted her about the phone call. They must have overheard her. Now, she felt compromised, and no longer wanted any part of this scheme. Why did she always fall for the wrong guy? It started when she flirted with Bobby Ringbottom, knowing he was Loretta's boyfriend and then about his deception with her sister, Madison. She should have known better than to fall for his good looks. It was unlikely he'd be any more faithful to her than he had been with them.

And then the circle of betrayal that included Cathy and Monica Bailey. What a group! So much hatred and revenge swirling among the five of them, and she dipped her toe in that cesspool of negative emotions, all for Bobby's attention. But he lied. He said he'd break up with Loretta. And then she learned he was hanging out with Madison and accidentally got her pregnant. He tried to convince her not to have the baby, but she refused, and then she ended up dead. Did Bobby kill her? Suspecting him made her afraid of him and grateful that he was sitting in jail right now.

When she looked up and saw Monica waiting to be seated, her heart pounded and her stomach tightened. She thought she was in jail alongside Bobby. Their eyes met, so she put on her hostess face, smiled, and seated Monica at her favorite table near the window.

"Here you go," she said, handing her a menu.

Monica gave her a crooked smile. "Any specials today?"

Lily ran through them, and Monica ordered the same thing she always did, a burger cooked rare, a side of potato salad, and a sweetened iced tea. It felt like Monica was trying to make her squirm after Lily tried to talk her out of doing anything to Autumn.

She walked away, glad to be out of Monica's toxic energy, dreading returning with her food. She'd get someone else to bring it, but they were short-handed, so that wasn't an option. Lily had to bring her a drink, so she brought the iced tea and put it down in front of Monica, but couldn't get away before Monica said, "Changing sides, are you?"

Startled, Lily said, "I want to do what's right, and stalking Autumn isn't fair. She hasn't done anything to you."

"She's friends with Amy Armstrong. That's enough."

Lily balled her fists and blurted, "No, it's not. I'm not helping you hurt people, so find someone else to do your bidding."

"Who said I was going to hurt her?" Monica said in a lilting voice.

She felt Monica's eyes on her back as she walked away.

Shaking, Lily wished she had Ray Reed's phone number. Instead, she dialed the Stroudsburg police station, not sure what she would tell them.

Bobby Ringbottom sat in a holding cell, ignoring his dinner of a dry turkey sandwich on white toast, a small cup of mayonnaise, and mushy French fries, barely salted and with no ketchup packet. He tried to breathe deeply, but the air stuck at the bottom of his throat. He worried about how much he'd shared with Lily Harding, thinking his plan would impress her, and she'd finally go out with him. Would she become a witness or an ally?

But then Madison Armstrong and Cathy Bailey got involved. Madison pushed Bobby to get rid of Loretta while Monica Bailey encouraged Cathy to do the same. Poor Loretta didn't have a chance. Breaking up with her would have been a nightmare, with both her sisters wanting her completely out of their lives. He could have walked away. He should have walked away. The look in her eyes when she realized they were all in it together sunk his heart, but it was too late. The event was in motion. He would have suffered injuries in the flurry of daggers and blood.

Looking back, Loretta was a pain, but no worse than the other two. Only Lily seemed kind enough to change the course of his life. Maybe she would have encouraged him to make better decisions. But with pending fatherhood, Madison never would have allowed that. In one sense, Madison's death liberated him. Then again, he was sitting in a jail cell, his freedom taken from him. They had taken Loretta's life, so karma seemed in full play.

The women were the ones who fulfilled their hateful goal, but he'd helped them. Without his daggers, without him luring Loretta into the car, this wouldn't have happened. Maybe it would've given everyone time to calm down and make a different choice. Maybe

Cathy would have just kicked Loretta out of her apartment and said the heck with the blackmail. Who cared if people found out that Harley was her father? Bobby suspected more people knew than they were saying. But he knew crazy Monica and her jealousy were behind Cathy's decision.

For Madison, she'd always hated her sister. He suspected she slept with him as some sort of competitive thing, revenge for whatever slight she thought Loretta made toward her. Bobby wasn't always clear about Madison's logic. It was her idea to dump the body in the lake. Her comment that it was Loretta's favorite place should have tipped him off. It was Madison's way of giving her sister one last poke in the ribs, other than with the dagger.

By the time Monica took the last bite of her burger, Detective John Conroy was in the doorway waiting to be seated. He asked for a table near the window, where Monica sat. She looked up and sneered.

"What are you doing here?"

"Getting a bite to eat. It's been a long day interrogating suspects and all." He smiled and sat in the chair facing her.

"I'm not in the mood for company."

"Don't you care that I'm investigating the death of your daughter, Cathy?"

Monica clenched her jaw and made no comment.

"How about giving me some idea of who might want to murder Cathy?"

She pressed her lips together, folded her arms, and yelled, "Bobby Ringbottom! Who else could it be?"

"What makes you think that, Ms. Bailey?"

Her anger got the best of her. "Because I told him to kill Loretta, and then he got greedy and took my Cathy, too!"

"So, this was all your idea?"

"Of course it was. Bobby is too stupid to think for himself."

Detective Conroy stood up and took out his handcuffs. "Monica Bailey, you're under arrest for conspiracy to commit murder."

"What? I didn't do anything! I told Bobby to do it!"

"You have the right to remain silent…"

Monica didn't. She protested all the way out the door as Lily breathed easier, knowing Monica was no longer a threat.

20

"It's nice not to worry about being followed or attacked," said Autumn, putting the finishing touches on their picnic lunch of tuna salad on toast, coleslaw, potato chips, and lemonade, with kibble and snacks for the pups.

"Yes, let's find a quiet spot and relax," said Ray, putting Chrissy and Ace into their harnesses. He folded a heavy blanket and draped it over his arm.

Autumn grabbed the picnic basket.

"What's going to happen to Bobby?"

"I'm not sure yet. They're still determining the role Bobby played in Loretta's murder, along with the other two. My guess is he'll be in jail as long as Monica. At least twenty years."

"It's frightening the way people hold resentment for so long their emotions get the better of them. They can't see a better solution than eliminating the person they feel is in their way," said Autumn.

"They were never really friends. Selfish people are unlikely to see alternatives or think about someone else's feelings."

"We only have a couple of days left up here. Where should we go?" asked Autumn, loading the basket into the SUV.

"How about a different lake? I heard Echo Lake has a sandy beach, and they allow dogs."

He typed the location into his phone and took off in the direction it instructed. They were there in ten minutes. The smell of pine and cedar trees perfumed the air. They had the beach to themselves. Water lapped the sandy shoreline. Ray spread the blanket, while autumn unhooked the fur babies from their restraints. They took off down the beach, Ace much faster than Chrissy, but she tried to keep up on her short little legs. Ace suddenly turned and ran at her, confusing her for a minute. When she got her bearings, she chased him again.

Ray plopped down on the blanket, the sand making a soft landing. "Feels like a beanbag chair."

"Wow, I haven't sat in one of those in years. Maybe we should get one."

"Yeah, for our mountain house." Ray smiled, watching the water and taking a bite of his sandwich.

"If you're serious, we could look south of here in lake communities. As much as I like it here, the murders wrecked it for me, even if we get a house on a different lake."

"Whatever you want. The whole point is to get a place where we can relax."

They sat in comfortable silence, watching the water and the pups. A male approached them from the direction of the parking lot. He took his time walking to where they sat. As he got closer, they recognized Danny Cole.

"Hey, Danny," said Autumn. "Want to join us?"

"Sure," he said, sitting on the blanket next to Autumn.

"Do you come to this lake often?" asked Ray.

"This is my first time."

Ray frowned as Autumn poured Danny a cup of lemonade.

"What made you come today?" asked Autumn.

"You were here."

"How did you know that?" Ray said, getting into a less vulnerable position.

"The tracker I put on your car."

Autumn's mouth dropped open. "Why would you do that, for goodness' sakes?"

"I have to make things right."

"Meaning?" Ray was on his knees.

"You spoiled my plan when you put Bobby safely in jail."

"But he was part of the group that killed Loretta!" Autumn handed him the cup.

Danny took a swig of lemonade. "Exactly. I loved Loretta! They killed her. Bobby told Lily Harding their plan, and she told me."

"You knew who did it? We could have used your testimony to catch them a lot faster," said Ray.

"What use would that be? They'd still be alive."

Ace charged back toward the blanket, barking, with Chrissy trying to catch-up.

Danny grabbed Autumn and had a knife to her throat before Ray could stop him.

"Keep that dog away from me!"

"Ace, come here!" yelled Ray.

Ace took his place next to Ray, who was now standing. Both looked ready to pounce.

"What if I took away the person you loved most? Would you want to kill me? That's how I feel!"

"Okay, let's stay calm. I get it. I'd feel the same way." Ray said and held out his hand in a stop position. "Tell me what happened."

"I knew how much Madison hated Loretta. She complained to me about it and how she slept with Bobby. They tried to make her think she was crazy. I saw Madison sitting on the porch of Harley's store after the murder. She had to be punished! I snuck into the woods and waited for her. It didn't take long. She was an easy target."

Ace growled.

"Keep him back!"

Ray put a hand down to keep Ace in his current position. If he attacked now, he could hurt Autumn, or Danny would cut her before Ace could bite him.

Chrissy gave a few sharp barks and started toward her mommy. Ray grabbed her and held her close. If Danny hurt Chrissy, Autumn would never get over it.

"What about Cathy?"

"I could tell she was getting paranoid after I killed Madison, so I needed help. I told Lily Harding that I wanted to surprise Cathy with a present to make her feel better, since she probably missed Loretta. Lily is such a sap. She believed me and called to tell me Cathy was leaving the restaurant. She hated Loretta even more than Madison did, so it was rewarding to watch her take her last breath."

"Pretty strategic, Danny. But you saved Bobby for last and missed your chance."

"You either get me in to visit Bobby, along with a weapon, or I take a substitute for that sleazebag. Like your lovely wife, here. It's a shame. You were always nice to me," Danny said to Autumn.

"But how did you get Bobby's daggers to leave evidence? You helped get him arrested."

"I climbed through the window and took them, then put them back. It was easy."

Ace was getting impatient, his stare boring through Danny, waiting for his chance.

"You're slick, I'll give you that," said Ray. "No one suspected you."

Suddenly, Danny's arm twisted behind him, and the knife dropped. "I did," said Detective John Conroy.

Autumn scrambled away from him and into Ray's arms. Ace pounced on Danny, pinning him to the ground and baring his pearly teeth. Saliva dripped onto Danny's face, daring him to move.

"Good boy, Ace!" shouted Officer Campos.

Ray called Ace away from Danny so Officer Williams could grab Danny by the back of the shirt and haul him to his feet. Christine Campos cuffed him, and the two officers hauled him away to the patrol car parked nearby.

Autumn held Chrissy tight while Ray held her.

"Took you long enough," Ray said.

"I had to get a confession first. You okay, Autumn?"

She nodded, clinging to Ray.

"Sorry, I didn't tell you the plan. We found the tracking device on our vehicle the night the officers were outside the house. I let John know we were coming here and to stay back until we could catch him. I recorded the entire confession on my phone." He pointed to his cell, hiding behind the picnic basket. "And then I remembered where I'd seen the wristwatch Danny wore. It belonged to Miguel. He must have stolen it when he killed him."

"Now the case is really closed. Thanks for all your help, Ray. It's been great working with you."

They shook hands. "Enjoy your lunch." John Conroy left the beach.

"I'm not sure I'm hungry anymore," said Autumn, shaking from adrenalin.

"Let's just sit here for a bit. You'll feel better once you've calmed down."

They sat back down on the blanket, Ray's right arm around Autumn's shoulder, his left arm around Ace, and Chrissy enveloped in Autumn's arms.

⚡ 21 ⚡

"You could have told me!" Autumn said, punching Ray in the arm. "I would have been on guard."

"That's why I didn't tell you. It had to look natural."

"Yes, my terror was definitely authentic." She threw a few more items into her suitcase.

"There was protection all around you. If things got out of control, I would have let Ace go sooner. I just didn't want you to get bitten in the process of him taking down Danny."

"I trust Ace more than Danny. He probably would have chewed off Danny's arm before hurting me."

"You're probably right," Ray conceded. "I'm glad we solved this case before leaving. It will be good to get home."

"Back to the grind, although this wasn't much of a break, anyway."

"What do you say we look at houses on the way home? Give Maureen a call. I'm sure she could lineup some properties. While you do that, I'll text Alison and Christine and let them know how much we appreciate their help and see if they would consider moving to Knollwood."

"I was hoping you'd say that. You need more women on the force, and they'd be perfect!" agreed Autumn.

Chrissy jumped up on the bed where the suitcases lay open and hopped into one, nestling herself down into the clothes folded there.

Autumn reached for her, gently petting her head. "We wouldn't go anywhere without you, sweetheart."

Ace leaped up on the bed and put his face in Ray's.

"Or you either, buddy," he said, hugging the big dog.

Acknowledgments

Many thanks to my friends at the Abington Police Department, Officers Christine Da Cunha and Alison Gontowski, for patiently answering endless questions about the reality of police work and the law enforcement community. You're both more impressive than any fictional character could ever be. Also, to Abington Patrol Officer S. Scott Scholl, Jr., for letting me wave him down after he pulled a car over in front of my house and helping me when I was stuck on a plot point.

To my trusted friend and first line reader, Maxine Ashcraft, for keeping me true to the plot and doing right by Chrissy, Autumn, Ray, and Ace. Thanks to Paula Shankle, a reader from Wyoming, who reminded me of the word "zoomies" to describe how pups run at full speed through the house. A shout out to her fur babies, Tundra and Isabella, too! And, deep gratitude to my readers, who give me a reason to keep creating.

About the Author

Diane Wing, M.A., is a multi-published author of dark fantasy fiction, cozy mysteries, magical realism, and enlightening non-fiction. Her work helps people see the magical, spiritual, loving side of life with a practical edge. Diane is an avid reader, bibliophile, lover of trees and animals, and a lifelong learner. She and her husband are pet parents to Lily, a Shih Tzu mix, and Chiquita, a Chihuahua.

Book Club Questions

1. If you were going to recommend this book to a friend, what would you tell them?

2. In your opinion, who is the main character in this book? Why?

3. Autumn and Ray waited over four months to start their honeymoon only to be sidetracked by a series of murders at a vacation resort. Autumn is exceptionally patient and supportive as they set aside their plans to assist the local police solve the crimes. If this happened to you on your honeymoon, how would you have reacted? Would you be willing to put your own interests on hold and assist your spouse/partner solve the crimes?

4. Chrissy, the Shih Tzu has an amazing and invaluable ability to connect with Autumn and share vital information about the crime scenes from a pup's perspective. Have you ever felt a deep, non-verbal communication with a pet? Can you describe what happened and how it made you feel?

5. What roles do Ace and Chrissy play in this book? Are they the stars of the story?

6. Did you suspect the identity of the murderer before the end? Who did you think was responsible? Why?

7. What was your first clue?

8. The relationships between the residents of the resort town were complicated, intense, clandestine, and deadly. Each had their own reasons to rationalize murder. Which characters did you feel had sufficient motive to kill? Who did you suspect & why did you suspect them?

9. Who was your favorite character in this story? Describe why you feel that way?

10. Who was your least favorite character? Why?

11. Were you surprised with the ending?

12. Was there anything different about this book than your typical
    murder mystery?

Note from author to book club participants: Thank you for reading
my book. I hope you have enjoyed the ongoing adventures of
Autumn, Ray, Chrissy, and Ace. I am grateful for your interest and
hope my words resonated with you as a pet lover. Let's keep the
conversation going. Join the *Chrissy's Cozy Mysteries Book Club* on
FaceBook at https://www.facebook.com/groups/1689604305165212.

Recipes Inspired by the Tall Tree Inn
Special thanks to Maxine and Doug Ashcraft

Classy Potato Salad

- 2 lbs Yukon Gold potatoes - chopped into small bite-sized chunks. Do not peel.
- 1 cup mayonnaise
- 1/4 cup Dijon or other favorite mustard
- 1/4 cup white wine vinegar
- 1/4 cup seasoned rice wine vinegar (Marukan or Kikkoman are best)
- 1/4 cup chopped fresh dill weed
- 1 large sweet yellow onion, thinly sliced
- 1/2 TSP ground black pepper
- 1 cup chopped fresh celery
- 2 TSP celery seed, lightly toasted
- 1/2 TSP Onion salt

Cook chopped potatoes in boiling water until tender, about 10 minutes. Drain and cool. Toast celery seed briefly in non-stick pan until fragrant. About 2 minutes on medium heat. In large bowl, mix mustard, mayo, and vinegars. Add celery, onion, and dill. Mix well. Add cooled potatoes. Garnish with chopped fresh parsley and paprika. Cover tightly with plastic wrap and chill 4 hours or more before serving. Best when refrigerated overnight.

Vegetable Melt:
Garden vegetables baked with Swiss on pita.

(I omitted the complicated Beurre Blanc. I think Hollandaise sauce would be better.)

- 2 large Portobello mushroom caps, clean and remove center stems

- 2 large slices Beefsteak tomato

- 1/4 cup sliced mushrooms white or Cremini

- 1/4 cup sliced sweet onion

- 1/2 clove crushed fresh garlic

- 1/2 cup tightly packed baby spinach

- 1-2 oz sliced Gruyere or Swiss Emmental cheese

- 1 raw egg, beaten - optional

- 1 TSP Italian seasoned breadcrumbs.

- Salt to taste

- Olive oil or clarified butter (Ghee) for cooking vegetable

- 2 Whole Pita breads

Sautee Portobello mushroom cap on both sides until tender. Set aside in metal pan to use for broiler finishing. Sautee sliced mushrooms, onions, and baby spinach until tender. Combine hot veggie sauté with beaten egg, if used, and breadcrumbs. Egg can be substituted for 1 oz Ricotta cheese. Set aside.

Preheat your broiler. Toast whole pita breads. Cut each in half. Put on serving plates. Fill large Portobello mushroom caps with combined filling. Top with tomato slice and cheese slice on top.

Broil stuffed mushroom cap under broiler until cheese is melted and bubbly. Plate stuffed mushroom and veggies with toasted Pita and serve with a side of Hollandaise sauce and your favorite salad. Makes 2 servings.

Autumn's Favorite Tuna Melt

- 2 thick slices sourdough bread or rolls
- 1 can water packed tuna
- 1/4 cup sliced sweet red or white onion
- 1/4 cup finely sliced celery1/4 cup mayonnaise
- 1 TSP finely chopped parsley
- 1 TSP stoneground mustard
- 1 TSP fresh lemon juice (Meyer lemon is best)
- 1/2 cup grated Sharp Cheddar or other favorite cheese
- Chopped green onions for garnish
- Salt and black pepper to taste

Preheat broiler. Combine all ingredients and set aside in refrigerator for ½ hour.

Lightly toast bread in toaster. Place on broiler pan and split tuna mixture in half. Place on toast and lightly pack down. Top with cheese slices. Place under hot broiler about three minutes or until cheese is melted and bubby.

Garnish with sliced green onions. Serve with your favorite salad.

Makes 2 open faced sandwiches

Moonlight Lake Coleslaw

- 4 Cups finely shredded or chopped fresh red cabbage
- 4 Cups finely shredded or chopped fresh green cabbage
- 1 Cup finely shredded or chopped carrots
- 1/2 Cup finely shredded or chopped red bell pepper or sweet peppers
- 1 1/2 Cups Mayonnaise
- 3/4 cup seasoned white rice vinegar (Marukan or Kikkoman are best)
- 1 TSP prepared horseradish 1/2 TSP ground white pepper

Combine all ingredients.

Garnish with chopped Italian parsley.

Makes 8 servings

Mediterranean Style Meatloaf
(for humans only!)

- 1 lb each of ground chuck, ground pork, and ground turkey
- 3 egg yolks
- 3/4 cup panko or Italian seasoned breadcrumbs
- 1 onion, finely chopped, and drained
- 2 T dried oregano
- 1 TSP teach of garlic powder, ground coriander, black pepper, pepper flakes, ground fennel seed
- 2 TSP sea salt.

Mix meat with spices, onion, mix in the egg yolks and panko. Form into a loaf shape on an oiled cookie sheet or large loaf pan. Let rest in the fridge for an hour. Bake in an oven @375* for 60 minutes, or until the internal temperature reaches 165*.

Makes 12 servings. Slice and serve with fresh mashed potatoes.

Meatloaf for Pups!

Combine meats, eggs, and breadcrumbs as above.

Do not add spices onion, or garlic.

Pups can have plain boiled potatoes with their "meatloaf".

Cooking directions same as above.

Ray Reed's Favorite Pub Burgers

Note: Use of cooking thermometer highly recommended

- 1 Lb Ground Beef (Wagyu or other grass-fed beef, chuck, or prime rib meat - 85% Lean / 15% Fat content)
- Salt and pepper
- 1 TBSP softened butter
- 1 TBSP BBQ dry rub seasoning of your choice
- 2 fresh potato rolls, split, toasted on a flat top or griddle
- 4 slices bacon, precooked to taste
- 2 - 1oz slices sharp cheddar or other favorite cheese
- Butter insides of potato buns and toast the buns

Loosely form 2 burger patties, 8oz each, sprinkle with salt and pepper, and the dry rub, and cook on medium high for approximately 3 minutes per side to an internal temperature of 150* for medium. Butter insides of potato buns and toast the buns. After second side of burger is done, add sliced cheese to each burger and cover lightly until cheese is melted - about 2 minutes.

Add garnishes: Choose from cooked bacon, avocado slices, lettuce, tomato slices, onion slices, pickle slices - plank or chips. Add your favorite condiments and dress the burgers!

In addition to traditional toppings like catsup, mustard, and mayonnaise, we highly recommend:

- Cajun Mayonnaise
- 1 cup mayonnaise
- 1/4 TSP ground cayenne pepper
- 1 TSP Tabasco sauce
- 1/2 TSP A-1 steak sauce

Combine all ingredients and refrigerate for at least two hours. Delicious! Try it with grilled chicken, turkey breast, or on a Rueben!

Grilled Cuban Sandwich:
Ham, Swiss, turkey, pesto, & pickle on Portuguese bread.

Preheat your Panini press or electric griddle.

- Four slices Cuban or Portuguese bread or two large soft sandwich rolls. Sweet French bread can be substituted

- 1/2 lb sliced Cuban roasted pork, if available, or maple glazed ham

- 1/4 lb sliced hot salami or capicola for extra zing

- Prepared pesto spread - optional.

- Two large dill pickles, sliced into thin planks

- 1/4 cup yellow or other favorite mustard

- 4 1 oz slices Swiss cheese

- Softened butter

Prep bread slices or opened sandwich rolls by buttering the outside of the bread and smearing mustard on the inside. If using pesto spread, place with mustard on inside of sandwich. Top mustard with cheese slices. Place half of the ham/capicola slices on each sandwich. Place sliced pickle planks on top of meats.

Close the sandwiches firmly and place in preheated Panini press or hot griddle. If using Panini press, cook covered with lid closed for about 5 minutes on medium high. If using a griddle, cook about 3 minutes on each side until bread is toasted and cheese is melted. Serve with your favorite salad.

Excerpt from "Attorney-at-Paw"

Ed. Note: we present this special excerpt from the very first Chrissy's Mysteries book for readers who did not have the opportunity to start the series at the beginning!

⚡ 1 ⚡

Squatting over a dead body was not Detective Raymond Reed's ideal lunchtime activity. The coroner estimated time of death as the night before around seven. It was almost one o'clock now. His stomach growled. The glare from the crystal chandelier hung high over the marble tile of Gary Martin's foyer bothered his eyes and made him cranky. Or maybe it was the fact that there were five officers and medical personnel working the scene and ignoring the little Shih Tzu shivering next to the body.

He stroked the pup's head before going through the dead man's pockets. He found gum, a receipt for the gum from a convenience store with a time and date stamp of yesterday evening at five fourteen, and his cell phone. His keys lay on the floor next to him.

Ray handed the phone to the officer closest to him.

"Sergeant, can you please see if you can find next of kin and put me on with them when you do?"

"Sure thing, Detective."

"Can you also find something to eat and drink for the dog? Maybe distract her with a toy?"

The sergeant nodded and went for the Shih Tzu, who backed up and growled in warning.

"I don't think she's interested, Detective."

Ray went out to his SUV and opened the hatch. His partner, German shepherd dog Ace, jumped out of the back and followed him into the house.

He knelt down next to Ace. "How about helping me with this little one, pal?"

Ace walked over to the Shih Tzu, who looked up at him towering over her. He gave her a little nudge. She held her ground. Ace let out a single bark, and the Shih Tzu stepped away from the body. Ace sat next to her.

Ray patted Ace and his charge on the head and went back to work. There were no apparent bruises or injuries on the body. He looked at the Shih Tzu.

"I wish you could tell me what happened here, little one."

Chrissy stared at him with an intensity that took him off guard.

"The victim's sister, Anna Martin, sir." The sergeant handed over the phone.

"Ms. Martin? This is Detective Raymond Reed of the Knollwood Police Department."

"Yes?" Ray noted her voice was filled with expectation and foreboding.

"I'm sorry to inform you that your brother was found dead in his home about an hour ago."

Ray listened for an emotional reaction but got only silence.

"Ms. Martin?"

"Yes. I'm just shocked at the news."

Ray heard annoyance rather than shock, as though her brother's death was an inconvenience rather than a tragedy.

"Ms. Martin, when was the last time you spoke to your brother?"

"Last week maybe. Why?"

"His dog was found alive sitting next to the body."

"Her name is Chrissy. That dog meant more to him than his own family."

Resentment and cool disgust landed in Ray's trained ear.

"Would you or your family like to come get her and identify the body?"

"I'll identify the body, but I don't want the dog. Send her to a shelter."

Being an animal lover and a dog owner himself, her reaction made him angry.

Controlling his voice, he said, "May we take her bedding and toys to the shelter also?"

"Whatever. I don't want any of that stuff."

Ray clenched his jaw.

"When are you available to come and identify the body?"

"I have to get my parents situated first. It will take about an hour to get there."

"I can meet you at the coroner's office at four this afternoon."

Anna sighed. "Fine." Ray heard a click, and she was gone.

Ray tucked the phone into the breast pocket of his suit jacket and looked at Chrissy.

"Chrissy," he said.

She looked at him.

"I'm sorry little one. We'll have to take you someplace where they'll take good care of you."

Her dark eyes shone with moisture, pulling at Ray's heartstrings.

"You don't want to go with your aunt anyway. Someone nice will come along."

Chrissy put her head down. Ace nuzzled her. Ray asked one of the officers to call Animal Control and instruct them to take Chrissy to a no-kill shelter.

"Can someone please gather all of Chrissy's belongings and put them in bags to go with her?"

He wished he could take her, but he had his hands full with Ace. He watched as a woman from Animal Control gently scooped her up and rubbed her back, while another staffer grabbed two bags of Chrissy's things. Chrissy looked over the woman's shoulder at Ray. When they turned, he saw her tail limp, and almost stopped them, but a strong instinct told him that something good would come out of this.

Back at the station, Ray gobbled a sandwich as he went through the address book of Gary's cell phone. Ace sat under his desk sharing bits of his lunch. Ray methodically made a list of those he wanted to question. Anna was at the top of the list, followed by Gary's partner, Vaughn Evans, and the woman who reported the death, Corinne Taylor.

Preliminary list complete, he called the shelter to make sure Chrissy had arrived and settled in. They reported that she would not eat or play. Ray was not surprised after everything she had been through.

Then he called Gary Martin's law office to find out about his will. A woman named Lisa Coleman answered. She told him the will was in probate and a matter of public record, so she gave him the beneficiary information.

He noted the time and headed over to the medical examiner's office to meet Anna Martin. She was already in the waiting area when Ray arrived, her sour expression contrary to the situation at hand.

"Ms. Martin?"

"Yes."

"I'm Detective Reed. We spoke on the phone."

"Right. Let's get this over with."

Ray showed her into an interview room.

"Where's the body?"

Ray noticed that she did not say "my brother."

"Please have a seat. I'd like to ask some questions that will give me a better picture of Gary."

"What for?"

"Please, Ms. Martin. This is standard procedure and your cooperation is appreciated."

She sat back and crossed her arms.

"May I have your address?"

She gave it to him with a curt tone.

"That's about an hour from here, correct?"

"Yes."

"When was the last time you spoke to Gary?"

"I told you before. It might have been last week."

"What did you talk about?"

"What we always talk about. I needed money to take care of my parents."

"Did Gary provide for them normally?"

"Not voluntarily. I always had to ask. Listen, I need to get back home."

"We're almost finished. How would you describe your relationship with the deceased?"

She chuckled. "Not great. We only spoke when we had to. Now I don't need to speak with him at all." Her mouth tightened to a thin line.

"Where were you day before yesterday around seven in the evening?"

"Home with my parents." She said without hesitation.

Ray nodded his head and made a note.

"Were you aware that you are the sole beneficiary in Mr. Martin's will?"

"Does that make me some kind of suspect?"

"What do you believe Mr. Martin died from?"

"How should I know? I'm not a doctor!" She waited a beat. "That's enough. Show me the body and let me get out of here."

Ray closed his notepad and showed her into the viewing room.

ဢ

Autumn Clarke shook off visions of the tractor-trailer grill filling the windshield and echoes of twisting metal, screams, and sirens. Toes curling in her shoes, she steadied herself against the brick wall and took a calming, deep breath that brought her back to the present. She looked around to see if anyone witnessed her episode. She hated when it happened in public places and desperately wanted to reclaim her self-control.

Panic subsiding, her focus shifted to the industrial glass doors that challenged her to enter with no promise of success. Autumn was afraid to love again, yet embers of hope glowed in the darkness and faith smoldered in her heart. This was the first step toward healing, and she opened to it like a folklorist drawn to an ancient fairy tale.

Her treatment plan had hit a wall. The nightmares of that fateful day crept into her waking consciousness. The recent rise in anxiety prompted her psychiatrist, Doctor Wesley Harper, to add this latest intervention. To heal, she needed to welcome love back into her life. So here she stood, despite intense skepticism and fear.

Taking a deep breath, she took a leap of faith with nothing to lose. She pulled open the glass door to the sterile, cinder block building, the smell of pungent disinfectant conjuring images of the hospital emergency room. Chest tight and tears glistening, she defied the urge to leave. The heels of her scuffed brown leather booties pounded the black and white tile floor and echoed off the bare walls up to the receptionist desk. The noise gave her courage somehow; it sounded strong and purposeful.

The wood-look laminate receptionist desk felt cold, yet the carrot-topped, curly-haired receptionist with the bright, friendly smile warmed the space. Her official clip-on tag revealed her name as Brenda.

"May I help you?"

Brenda wore a bright yellow T-shirt emblazoned with an illustration of a small, furry dog of no particular breed wearing a halo and the call to action: *Adopt a Fuzzy Angel Today.*

"Hi Brenda, I'm here to adopt a fuzzy angel."

Autumn and Brenda shared a smile, and Autumn's tension subsided.

"I'm happy to help you with that."

"I'm Autumn Clarke. I filled out the adoption application form on your website. Six pages' worth."

"We want to be sure that our fur babies go to the best homes," Brenda said as she typed Autumn's name into the computer system. "Here you are. Yes, your application is approved."

"I'd like a small breed, under 20 pounds."

"Wonderful! The sweetest little girl came in this afternoon. Right this way. She's a Shih Tzu."

Brenda led her down a drab, narrow hallway, wide hips swaying under the form-fitting T-shirt, and into the caged area. It was depressing to see these beautiful furry faces staring with soulful eyes from behind bars. Autumn wondered how big a heart was required to work here and stay strong. The stories she read on the shelter's website of how they got here were as sad as their expressions. They reminded Autumn of herself, caged by the memory of a fatal accident that haunted her day and night.

Their desperation, and her own, bounced off the walls and echoed back like a lonely coyote's cry in a canyon. Some dogs barked with loud and frantic tones. Others kept to themselves, withdrawn in uncertainty for the future. Autumn tried not to think about it and to focus on the one she was here to see.

Having a pet had never occurred to her. In all of the wonderful experiences her parents had brought her, none included a pet of any kind. Not even a fish. So, now to be responsible for the wellbeing of a dog made her hands go clammy and her heart race.

The idea of entering into a relationship seemed foreign. The *Land of Connection* was a place she had visited long ago and could only recall pieces of the trip. She was afraid of attachment. She worried that her treatment plan would not work. She dreaded being alone forever. Despite intense skepticism and fear, to heal, she needed to welcome love back into her life.

Her personal default was to research whatever challenge she faced or topic she wrote about as a freelance journalist. She'd spent several evenings poring over the massive amount of information online about what it is like to have a dog before following her doctor's suggestion and making the decision to adopt. She learned what a huge undertaking it is to have a pet; her choice to show up anyway demonstrating the commitment to her healing and improving the life of a little dog in the process.

Still, her stomach tightened at the thought of having an animal in the house. She used Dr. Wes' trick of feeling her feet on the floor and focusing her attention on Brenda, noting every movement she made to keep her mind occupied. His methods were effective, albeit non-traditional at times. That was what she liked most about him. The latest suggestion forced her to step out of her comfort zone and tackle this latest challenge.

"Here she is." Brenda petted the little dog through the bars.

The moment the Shih Tzu lifted her angelic face and stared straight into Autumn Clarke's eyes, she knew this little cutie was coming home with her. The sad, dark eyes looked at Autumn through tangled white bangs. The one stuffed toy in her cage went ignored. This little dog reflected Autumn's own sorrow and loss of hope.

Dr. Wes's idea to get an emotional support dog as complementary treatment might work out after all. A glimmer of hope sparkled in the dark place that had become her world, for herself and for this precious treasure.

"Her name is Chrissy. She's three years old," said Brenda. Chrissy gave the softest wave of her tail, and Autumn stuck her fingers through the bars of the cage. Chrissy sniffed and then nuzzled Autumn's hand. The dog was white and charcoal gray with a tuft of white like a halo over her forehead.

"She's so adorable. How did she end up here?"

"Her pet parent died yesterday," Brenda said. "He lived alone and Chrissy sat next to his body overnight, until a friend found them and called 911."

Autumn gasped.

"How did he die?"

"From what I hear, a heart attack."

She connected with Chrissy's circumstances, her own parents lost to her in a sudden, tragic accident three months earlier. Autumn was the only survivor. She leaned closer and whispered, "Poor baby!" Chrissy blissfully closed her eyes and pressed into Autumn's fingers. For the first time since the accident, Autumn felt warmth in the spot where her heart had ached with cold. Maybe Dr. Wes was right. Maybe she and Chrissy could help each other.

"I'm surprised no one took her in."

"The family had no interest in taking her, so animal control brought her to us."

Chrissy now paid attention, her eyes alert, seeming to know they were talking about her.

Brenda continued, "You should know that Shih Tzus were bred as companion animals, so they are affectionate lap-dogs who love to be loved and to give love. Because of that, this breed is prone to separation anxiety, and her recent experience exacerbated that, so she has severe separation anxiety. I've been spending as much time with her as I can since she came in. She shakes uncontrollably when left alone."

"Who doesn't," mumbled Autumn.

"Excuse me?"

"Nothing."

"Are you still interested? Most people don't want to deal with that kind of issue."

"I don't mind. I work from home, so there's no need for us to be separated."

Autumn didn't let Brenda know that Chrissy was destined to be an emotional support animal, able to accompany her everywhere. It was embarrassing to show weakness, especially to strangers. Her father had taught her to be strong, and part of her felt guilty for dropping the ball on that lesson.

Brenda opened the cage door. The button nose surrounded by long, white hair captured Autumn, the joy and affection expressed in a broad smile she had lost along with her parents. Chrissy was cuter than a stuffed animal, her intent stare of anticipation emanating from her white and gray face.

Autumn reached in and pulled Chrissy out, cuddling her against her chest. Chrissy rested her head on Autumn's shoulder, sorrow and relief pouring from her small body in little tremors. She gave her a loving squeeze and stroked her head. Chrissy grunted and sighed. Thinking about helping this little girl opened Autumn's heart and filled it with tenderness.

"She's perfect," she said to Brenda, and then to Chrissy, "Want to come home with me?"

Chrissy cooed on cue, and snuggled against Autumn.

Autumn closed her eyes, savoring the delightful feeling of Chrissy's head, so trusting against her neck. "Where do I sign?"

A half hour later, Autumn strolled out of the shelter with her new furry friend and two kitchen-sized trash bags full of everything a well-cared-for Shih Tzu needs: clothes, lots of toys, two doggie beds, harnesses, bowls, leashes, brushes, and bows gathered from her former home by the police.

"Boy, your daddy loved you! You have so many nice things."

Chrissy looked up at Autumn, acknowledging the truth of this statement, a hint of a smile on Chrissy's little black lips.

Autumn lifted her onto the soft, pink blanket covering the pristine beige leather backseat of the silver Mercedes SUV. Chrissy cooperated and settled onto the blanket, her tail wrapped around the side of her body. Autumn petted her head and closed the car door. She opened the hatch and threw the bags into the back.

The Mercedes was part of Autumn's inheritance and kept her parents close to her. She and her mother had food-shopped in it and took trips to the mall, loading the spacious back with their finds. Riding in it soothed the persistent anxiety marking Autumn's life since the death of her parents, Stella and George Clarke.

Her parents had been the biggest part of her world. She shared with them joys, sorrows, successes, and missteps; all experiences met with equal attention and trusted counsel. In her twenty-eight years of life, they were never too busy to listen or to share the major and minor moments of Autumn's life. She accompanied them to charitable events and to dinner parties. Friends were welcomed with open arms, and gatherings were celebrations of love and life. Their home was happy and peaceful in general, with rare times of angst.

Autumn glanced at her new charge curled up on the blanket, her heart fluttering. She smiled when Chrissy lifted her head to gaze back at her with a slight tilt of her head. She reached between the seats and scratched Chrissy's ears, and then pulled the seatbelt across her chest.

Autumn checked her rearview mirrors and inched out of the parking space. A red flash alerted her to the fast approach of a car. Autumn's foot stomped the brake, jarring Chrissy in the backseat. She flung her hand to steady the little body and watched the car zoom past.

Autumn's breath caught, along with her seatbelt. The seatbelt tightened in the same way as when the tractor-trailer had slammed head-on into her parents' Audi, killing them both and sparing Autumn, who was riding in the backseat. The sensation settled in, triggering hyperventilation and paralysis. She heard Chrissy growling in the distance. Face numb, she fought to refocus on the present, but the memories persisted.

They had been on their way to a fundraiser supporting her mother's work with an organization addressing drug abuse and addiction in Bucks County. The opioid-filled truck driver who had lost control of the truck proved the need for the foundation.

Chrissy's growls turned to insistent barks, bringing Autumn back from the shadows of the past. She reached back and gave Chrissy a loving squeeze.

"What a smart girl! I'm okay now, sweetheart."

Chrissy grunted and sighed.

Autumn took a few deep breaths to regroup.

"Let's go shopping!"

Taking another long, cautious look around the parking lot, Autumn pulled out and headed to the local pet superstore.

Chrissy perked up as they entered through the sliding automatic doors. Everyone who passed her smiled or reached out to pet her. She reveled in the attention, giving a wag when people made a fuss. Chrissy walked over to the freezer section, sat down in front of the shelf, and looked at Autumn.

"Really? You know what type of food this is?"

Chrissy beat her tail against the floor and licked her lips. Autumn held up various food choices until Chrissy gave a single bark indicating the one she wanted. They did the same with snacks and toys. Chrissy chose a small, blue ball and a bright pink stuffed piggy with a squeaker inside. Autumn shook her head, watching the way Chrissy made decisions. It was endearing and a little eerie at the same time.

Thinking of the sudden stop she had made in the rescue shelter parking lot, she bought the most secure, comfortable pet seat they had. The red lining with tan outer material coordinated with the beige interior of the Mercedes.

At the car, Autumn removed the pet safety seat from the bag and put the rest of Chrissy's things in the hatchback. She reached down to put Chrissy in the front seat while she dealt with installing Chrissy's new perch. It only took a few minutes to set up, line it with the pink blanket, and plop Chrissy in.

"There, safe and sound. Comfy?"

Chrissy made a little snorting sound. Autumn shook her head and caressed Chrissy's face in adoration. She wondered if all dogs were this aware.

With both hands on the wheel to ensure ultimate control of the vehicle, she drove the short distance through light traffic on the main roads, past the Giant supermarket and the medical center and onto the peaceful, tree-lined street of Acorn Lane. Dappled sunlight permeated the canopy of green that shaded pedestrians, drivers, and kids on bikes.

She drove past well-kept lawns and box-shaped Japanese holly bushes that filled her mind with happy childhood memories. Her family's Bucks County farmhouse made of Pennsylvania fieldstone and wood sat on almost two acres of land. The privacy it afforded was one of her mother's favorite aspects of the house, while Dad liked the solid warmth of the stone and plaster. His favorite comment about the house, "They don't build them like this anymore," echoed in Autumn's mind.

The divided light windows and doors, painted weathered navy blue, brought out the nineteenth century elements of the building. The home renovation was a labor of love her parents had undertaken in detail, keeping the historic ornamentation while modernizing the electric, plumbing, and kitchen. It was comfortable and inspiring, her imagination sparked by the Nancy Drew books she had read as a child sitting in the window seat of the library room. Fond memories of her parents lingered reading her stories aloud and encouraging her to write and her outdoor adventures in the neighborhood.

The house and everything in it belonged to her now. Despite her financial wealth, she would rather have her parents than their things.

She took a deep breath and clicked the garage door opener. She looked at Chrissy to see if she reacted to the noise of the motor. Chrissy was perfectly calm and met Autumn's eyes, telling her she was fine with it.

Now I'm thinking this dog can tell me things. Am I not crazy enough as it is?

Autumn rolled the car into her mother's side of the two-car garage. The windshield hit the tennis ball hanging from the ceiling, and she closed the door behind them. Dad had installed this safeguard after Mom overshot the length of the garage and scraped the front bumper while causing a dent in the garage wall and Mom's ego. They teased her about it whenever possible. The dent remained, and tore at the nick in her heart each time she saw it. She thought about getting it fixed but the thought of doing so threatened to erase a part of the relationship she had with her parents.

Her own bluish-silver Prius sat parked in her father's spot. The insurance company totaled the twisted heap of metal that was his Audi after the accident.

Thoughts of her dad pulling into the garage after a long day at his thriving accounting firm flooded her mind. George Clarke taught his daughter to be strong, to have a will, and to persist when the going got tough. She had let him down. Hands gripping the wheel, she sat there, silent tears flowing down her cheeks. She whispered "Miss you," and grabbed a tissue from the ever-present box next to her. Another deep breath and she stepped out of the car.

She lifted Chrissy from her car seat and put her on the floor, removing the leash and guiding her through the entry door into the laundry room adjacent to a kitchen any chef would enjoy. Her mother, Stella, loved to cook, and the six-burner Viking stove, pale maple cabinets, and travertine backsplash reflected quality design and a love of feeding her family.

Stella flourished in her domestic role, happy to sew, clean, and cook, while running successful fund raising events for The Advocates of Southeast Pennsylvania, a group dedicated to prevention, intervention, and addiction recovery solutions. Her mother's interest in this particular nonprofit rose from losing her cousin to opioid addiction.

Chrissy sniffed the doorframe and the floor before padding into the kitchen of her new home. Autumn followed with the bags of goodies from the pet store and the shelter. She washed Chrissy's bowls, filled one with filtered water, and placed them on the floor on a cloth placemat bordered with flowers. Chrissy drank with gusto, lifted her dripping chin, and looked at Autumn with thanks, her black lips curving into a smile. She ambled over to the sliding glass doors that led to a patio and fenced yard.

"Outside? Glad you're housetrained."

Autumn slid open the door and Chrissy stepped across the threshold. She sat on the patio and checked out her new, fenced yard and lush green surroundings. She walked over to the thick lawn, relieved herself, and then came right back to Autumn. Never having had a dog before, she did not know quite what to expect, and wondered if this was normal. Were all dogs this cooperative and laid-back? Did they all have the ability to convey exactly what they wanted? If not, she had certainly lucked out in finding Chrissy.

Autumn grabbed an iced tea and she and Chrissy sat outside together. The late spring afternoon was sunny and pleasant, birds chirping and squirrels scampering in the yard. This was Stella Clarke's favorite time of year, anticipating the cycle of blossoms that added seasonal beauty to the garden. Autumn petted Chrissy, who accepted the attention and pushed her head against her hand. She looked up at Autumn with watery eyes that were deeper than any human's she'd ever encountered.

"You miss your daddy?"

Chrissy stared back in response.

"I know. I miss mine, too."

They understood each other's pain. Autumn picked up her new friend and snuggled her between her outstretched legs so she could see the birds and squirrels enjoying the leafing sycamore and maple trees. Chrissy settled in, the sun and the warm spring breeze gently touching Autumn's skin and ruffling Chrissy's hair. Autumn's body released tension for the first time since losing her parents. Chrissy let out a deep sigh. They both closed their eyes and took a much-needed nap.

The Adventures of Autumn and Chrissy Begin Here!

Only Chrissy, a cute little Shih Tzu, can unlock this mystery! Autumn Clarke survived the car crash that killed her parents. To help her cope with PTSD, she adopts Chrissy, a Shih Tzu with a remarkable secret. Chrissy is also the only witness to the mysterious death of her pet parent. Autumn vows to find the truth behind his death with the help of Chrissy, the neighbors and an attractive detective. Can Autumn unravel the clues while trying to heal Chrissy's trauma and overcome her own devastating emotional wounds in the midst of a dangerous murder investigation?

"Chrissy the Shih Tzu may be the cutest sleuth on the job, but don't let that button nose fool you—it's perfectly able to sniff out a killer with a little help from her human friends. Great start to a fun new series!"

—Sheila Webster Boneham, Author of the award-winning *Animals in Focus Mysteries*

"Diane Wing does an excellent job of showing readers just how animals can communicate with us through images and actions when we are tuned into their frequency. Through the relationship between Autumn and Chrissy, Wing also shows the importance of therapy animals and how much they can help those who need them. Add in a sweet romance to the intrigue of the mystery and you've got a book that you won't want to put down."

—Melissa Alvarez, Intuitive, animal communicator and author of *Animal Frequency* and Llewellyn's *Little Book of Spirit Animals*

"Diane Wing has created a wonderfully endearing little character in Chrissy the Shih Tzu. It really shines through that the author is an animal and dog lover. I can see these books quickly becoming a cherished addition to the cozy mystery genre."

—J. New, author of *The Yellow Cottage Vintage Mysteries*

Learn more at www.DianeWingAuthor.com

From Modern History Press

In this 2nd installment in the series, Chrissy digs up clues to help Autumn solve a historical disappearance and a modern-day murder mystery

Autumn Clarke is getting her life back to normal with the help of her extraordinary Shih Tzu, Chrissy, when the death of a local philanthropist reveals the man's dark family secrets, as well as unexpected ties to Autumn. When Chrissy discovers a dog-eared diary in the dead man's family home, Autumn discovers that things in the Clarke family are not quite as they seem. Can Autumn interpret the hidden clues in the dog-eared diary to crack the most puzzling disappearance in Knollwood history? Are the recent murders connected to the past? Is Chrissy more insightful than Autumn realized?

"I have fallen in love with Chrissy and Autumn and their continuing journey to health while finding themselves in the middle of a murder mystery adventure. My pre-teen daughter and I enjoyed reading *The Dog-Eared Diary* and then discussing the clues, plot twists, and characters."

—Antoinette Brickhaus, Maryland

"Chrissy the Shih Tzu is a real character in the book and not just a prop to help the story along. Chrissy often felt like she was going to start talking. I loved the relationship between Autumn and her dog. The love the two of them have is absolutely perfect. Perfect for a rainy afternoon and one any cozy mystery fan will enjoy. I can't wait to see what happens next!"

—Andrea J. Guy

"I applaud the author for her use of so many clever writing devices within a rather brief cozy mystery. Nothing seemed contrived nor out-of-place. I hope that someone makes the decision to adapt these books to the screen because it would make one amazing mystery series!"

—Ruth A. Hill, journalist

Learn more at www.DianeWingAuthor.com

From Modern History Press

Prepare to be tricked & treated in this 3rd installment of the Chrissy the Shih Tzu cozy mysteries!

Fall has arrived in Knollwood, and Autumn Clarke is planning an elaborate Halloween event at The Peabody Mansion B&B to support the local animal shelter. With the entire town invited and the inn not officially open for overnight guests, an unexpected request lands Dana Wood, an A-list actor, as a long-term guest while shooting her latest movie in New Hope. Autumn and the gang step in to help with her baggage filled with betrayal, scandal, unsolved murder, a personal secret, and a cast of eccentric, suspicious characters. As the filming begins, Chrissy's shrewd judge of character and nose for unearthing incriminating evidence provide the backdrop for this twisty and thrilling tale.

Bonus features: book club questions, recipes of meals from the book, and a Halloween scavenger hunt list appear at the end of the book!

"Autumn and Chrissy have become my favorite crime solvers!! Diane Wing has put together another fun rainy afternoon, cuddle-with-my-dog in-a-corner-window mystery! Throughout this series we have seen Autumn and Chrissy overcome tragedy, find love, and solve some murders! All her supporting characters make sense and are loveable. A great read for anyone from 8 to 80!!"

—Antoinette B., Leonardtown, MD

"*Trick-or-Doggy-Treat* is a delightful, satisfying cozy mystery wrapped in the rich, colorful tapestry of a Pennsylvania fall in a wonderful town. Halloween has never been this enchanting. A truly enjoyable read!"

—Maxine Ashcraft, Oakland, CA

Learn more at www.DianeWingAuthor.com

From Modern History Press

The Perfect Wedding..... *Cursed?*

In this 4th installment of the *Chrissy the Shih Tzu* cozy mysteries, Autumn Clarke and Ray Reed are planning the winter wedding of the year, and the first major social event at Autumn's newly renovated Peabody Mansion Bed & Breakfast. Autumn's dreams are about to come true—a spectacular, romantic ceremony with the handsome love of her life. After their beloved Shih Tzu, Chrissy, discovers the body of a popular local psychologist in a snowdrift weeks before the wedding, a series of unexplainable setbacks begin to foil their wedding plans. Is it deliberate sabotage, or is the wedding truly cursed? Will dangerous, uninvited guests create matrimonial mayhem and ruin their special day? Wing's Cozy fans can expect an exciting, romantic whodunit with an abundance of twists and turns that will keep them on the edge of their seats until the very last page is turned.

"Treat yourself to *A Winter's Tail*--the latest gripping addition to Diane Wing's wildly popular *Chrissy's Mysteries* cozy series. Things turn dark and strange as Autumn encounters a series of bizarre and shocking events before their wedding day. Are the nuptials really cursed, or is it a vengeful foe returning for the ultimate revenge and desecration of Autumn and Ray's happily ever after? Snuggle in for this delightful treat."

—Maxine Ashcraft, Oakland, CA

"This installment of the *Chrissy the Shih Tzu* cozy mysteries finds Chrissy's pet parent, Autumn, preparing for her wedding to Ray Reed, a local police lieutenant. Autumn's friend and cousin, Bea, is worried that Autumn and Ray's nuptials are cursed because of several setbacks to Autumn's plans. Meanwhile, Chrissy discovers a body in a snow pile and Ray is assigned to investigate the victim's death. This is the best book of the series so far! I couldn't figure out who was sabotaging Autumn and Ray's wedding until the final reveal. A fun, cute, and enjoyable read. "

—Terri Chalmers, Sicklerville, NJ

Learn more at www.DianeWingAuthor.com

Dark Fantasy from Diane Wing

Indulge your Imagination!